Some of m... ...d reviews:

'Will make you
augh out loud,
ringe and
nigger, all at
he same time'
LoveReading4Kids

**Waterstones
Children's
Book Prize
Shortlistee!**

SCHOLASTIC
Lollies
LAUGH OUT LOUD
BOOK AWARDS
**PRIZE-WINNING
AUTHOR**

'**WHAT'S
NOT TO
LOVE?**'
—Sun

'Very
funny
and
cheeky'
—Booktictac,
Guardian Online Review

'I LAUGHED
SO MUCH, I
THOUGHT THAT
I WAS GOING
TO BURST!'
Finbar, aged 9

The review of the eight
year old boy in our house...
Can I keep it to give to a friend?"
Best recommendation you
can get' - Observer

'HUGELY
ENJOYABLE,
SURREAL
CH...
—Gu...

I am still not a Loser
The Roald Dahl
**FVNNY
PRIZE** 2013

First published in Great Britain in 2015
as Barry Loser's ultimate book of keelness!
by Egmont UK Ltd

This updated edition published in 2019
by Egmont UK Ltd, The Yellow Building,
1 Nicholas Road, London W11 4AN

Text and illustrations copyright © Jim Smith 2015, 2019
The moral rights of Jim Smith have been asserted.

ISBN 978 1 4052 8712 8

barryloser.com
www.egmont.co.uk

A CIP catalogue record for this title is available from the British Library

Printed and bound in Great Britain
by the CPI Group

70108/001

EGMONT
We bring stories to life

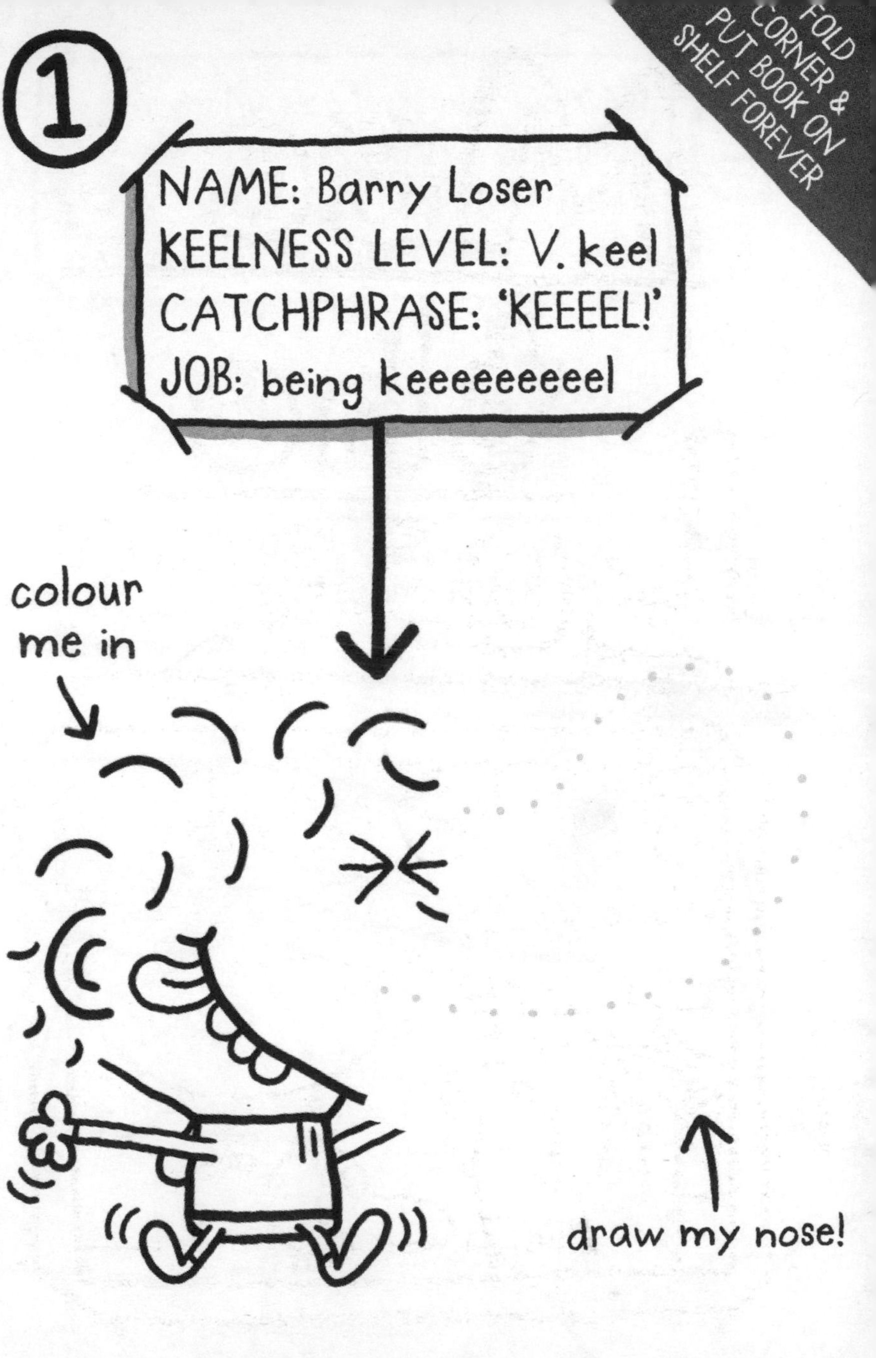
FOLD CORNER & PUT BOOK ON SHELF FOREVER
1
NAME: Barry Loser
KEELNESS LEVEL: V. keel
CATCHPHRASE: 'KEEEEL!'
JOB: being keeeeeeeeeel
colour me in
draw my nose!

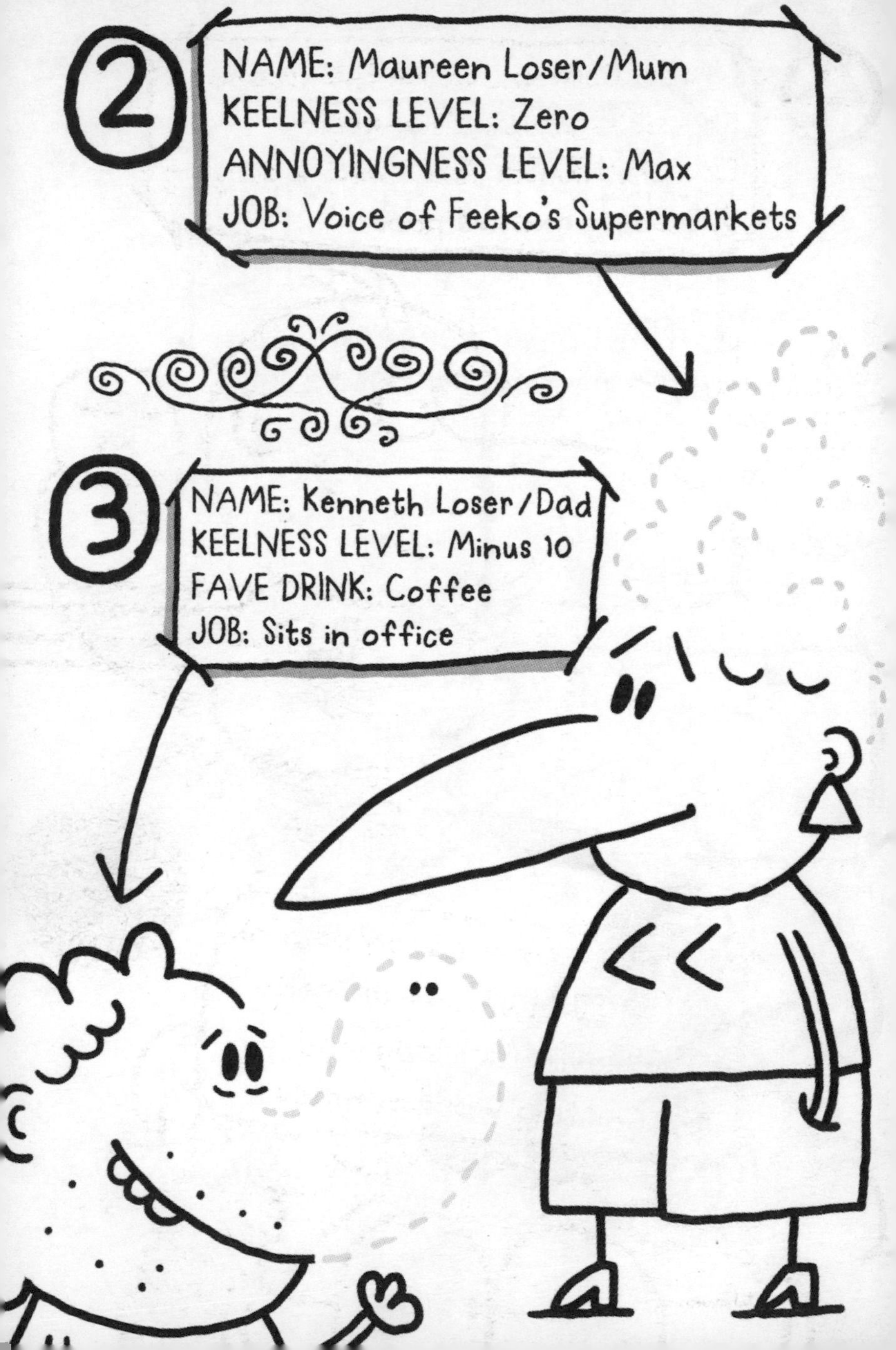

2
NAME: Maureen Loser/Mum
KEELNESS LEVEL: Zero
ANNOYINGNESS LEVEL: Max
JOB: Voice of Feeko's Supermarkets
3
NAME: Kenneth Loser/Dad
KEELNESS LEVEL: Minus 10
FAVE DRINK: Coffee
JOB: Sits in office

4

NAME: Desmond Loser the Second
KEELNESS LEVEL: Mini-keel
CATCHPHRASE: Screaming & gurgling
JOB: Doing massive poos

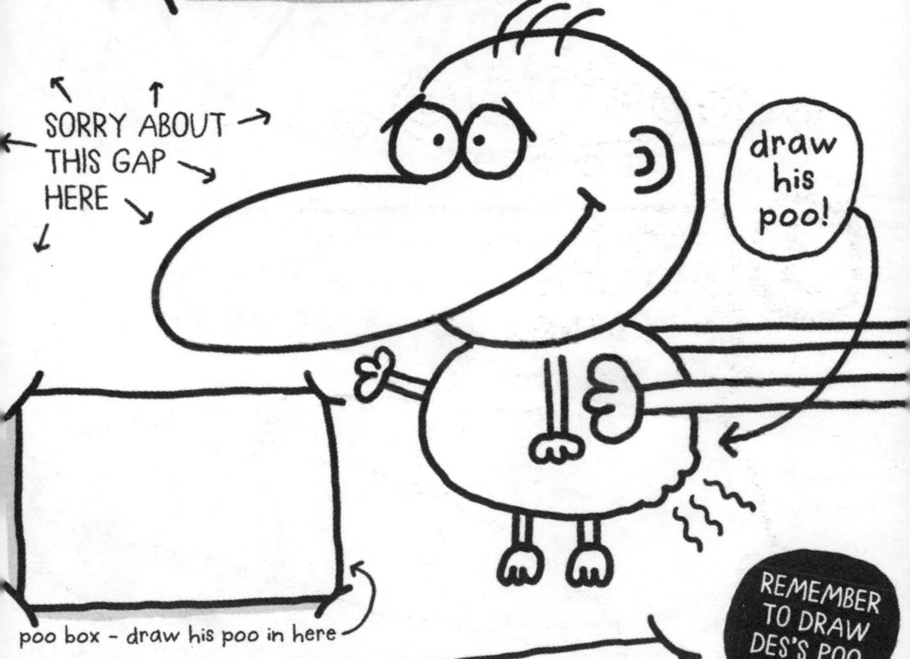
SORRY ABOUT THIS GAP HERE
draw his poo!
poo box - draw his poo in here
REMEMBER TO DRAW DES'S POO, GUYS!

5

NAME: Granny Harumpadunk
KEELNESS LEVEL: Grannyish
BOYFRIEND: Mr Hodgepodge
JOB: Knitting woollen noses

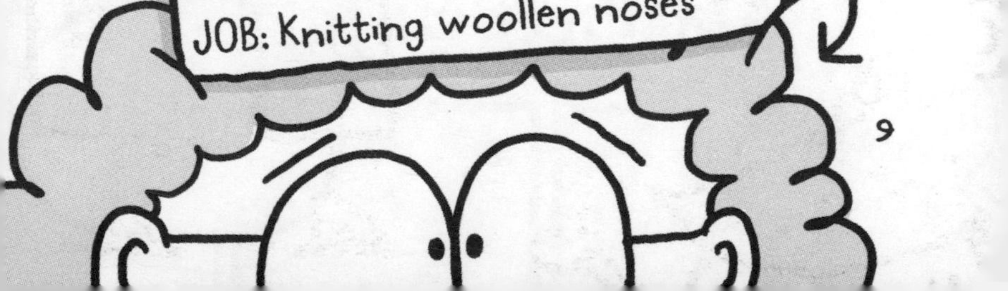

Talk like a Loser

EEVE KEELSE

of course

Me and Bunky think we're SOOO keel, saying our made-up words. Here's what they mean...

when you're all relieved about something

Keel!

cool

thank keelness

salute the keelness!

if you see something keel and want to salute it

add this on to the end of a word to make it more loseringtons

unkeel

-ingtons

DINNER DAMES

uncool

dinner ladies

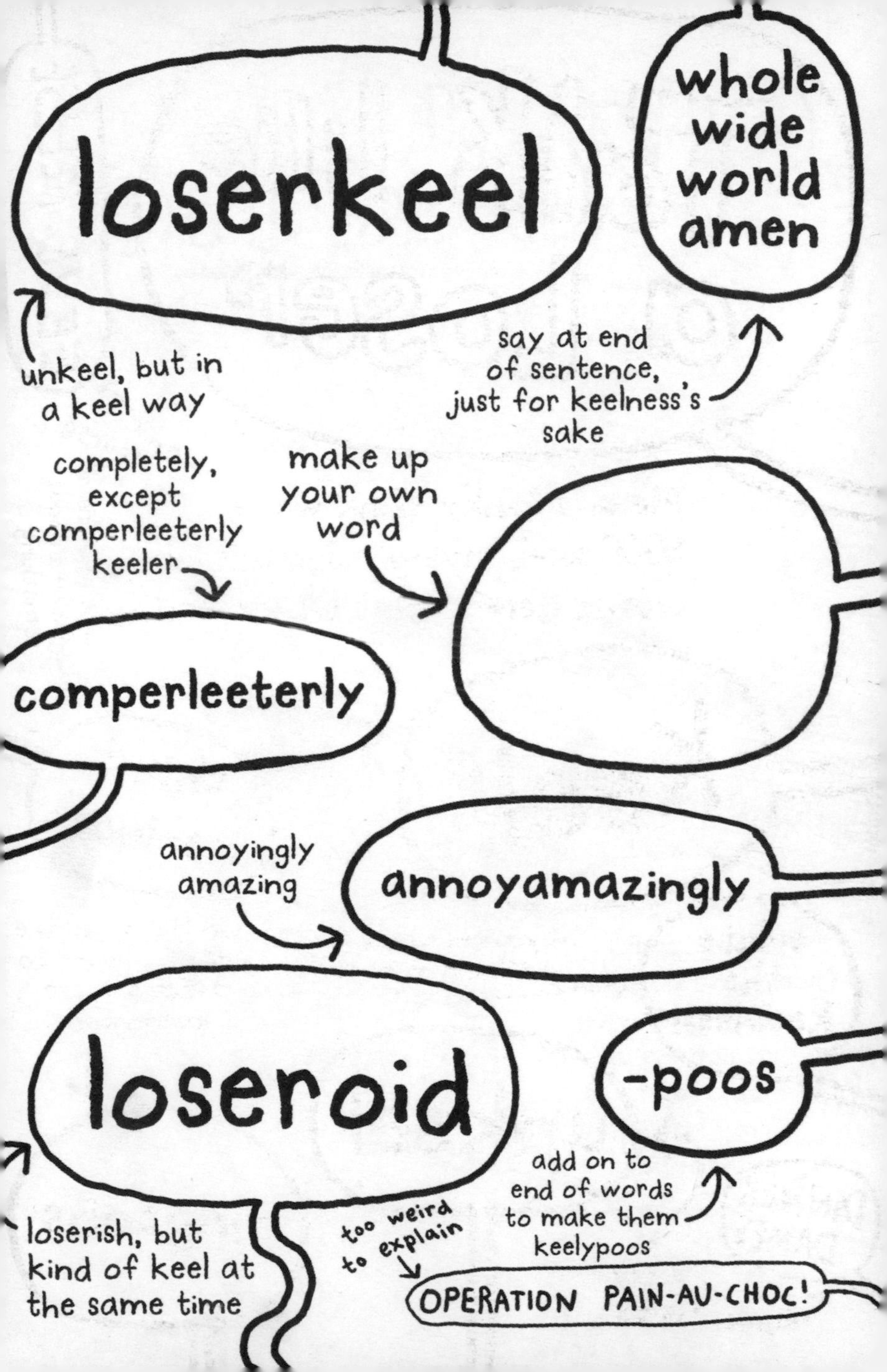
loserkeel
unkeel, but in a keel way
whole wide world amen
say at end of sentence, just for keelness's sake
completely, except comperleeterly keeler
comperleeterly
make up your own word
annoyingly amazing
annoyamazingly
loseroid
loserish, but kind of keel at the same time
-poos
add on to end of words to make them keelypoos
too weird to explain
OPERATION PAIN-AU-CHOC!

Sketches

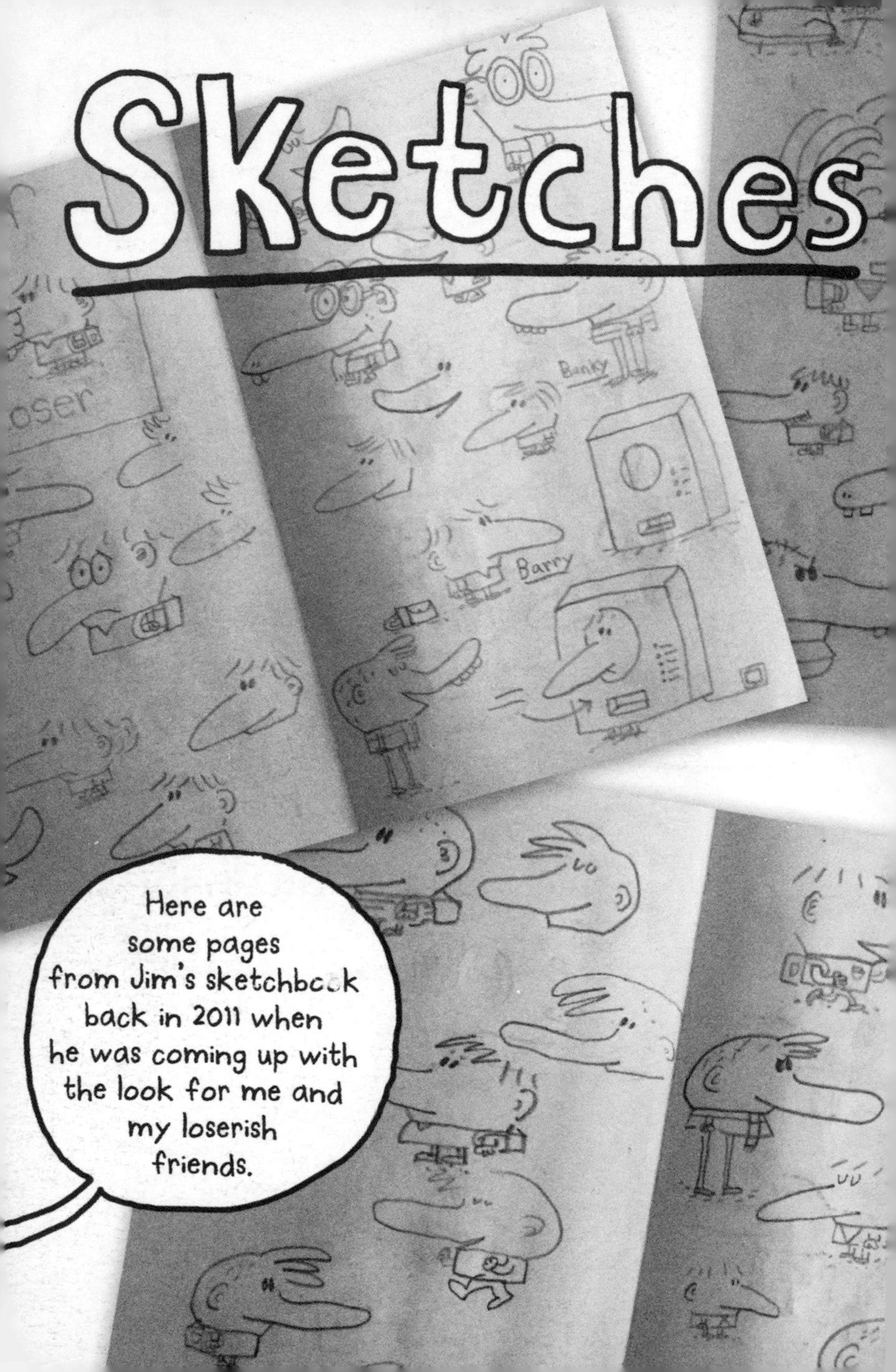

Here are some pages from Jim's sketchbook back in 2011 when he was coming up with the look for me and my loserish friends.
Banky
Barry

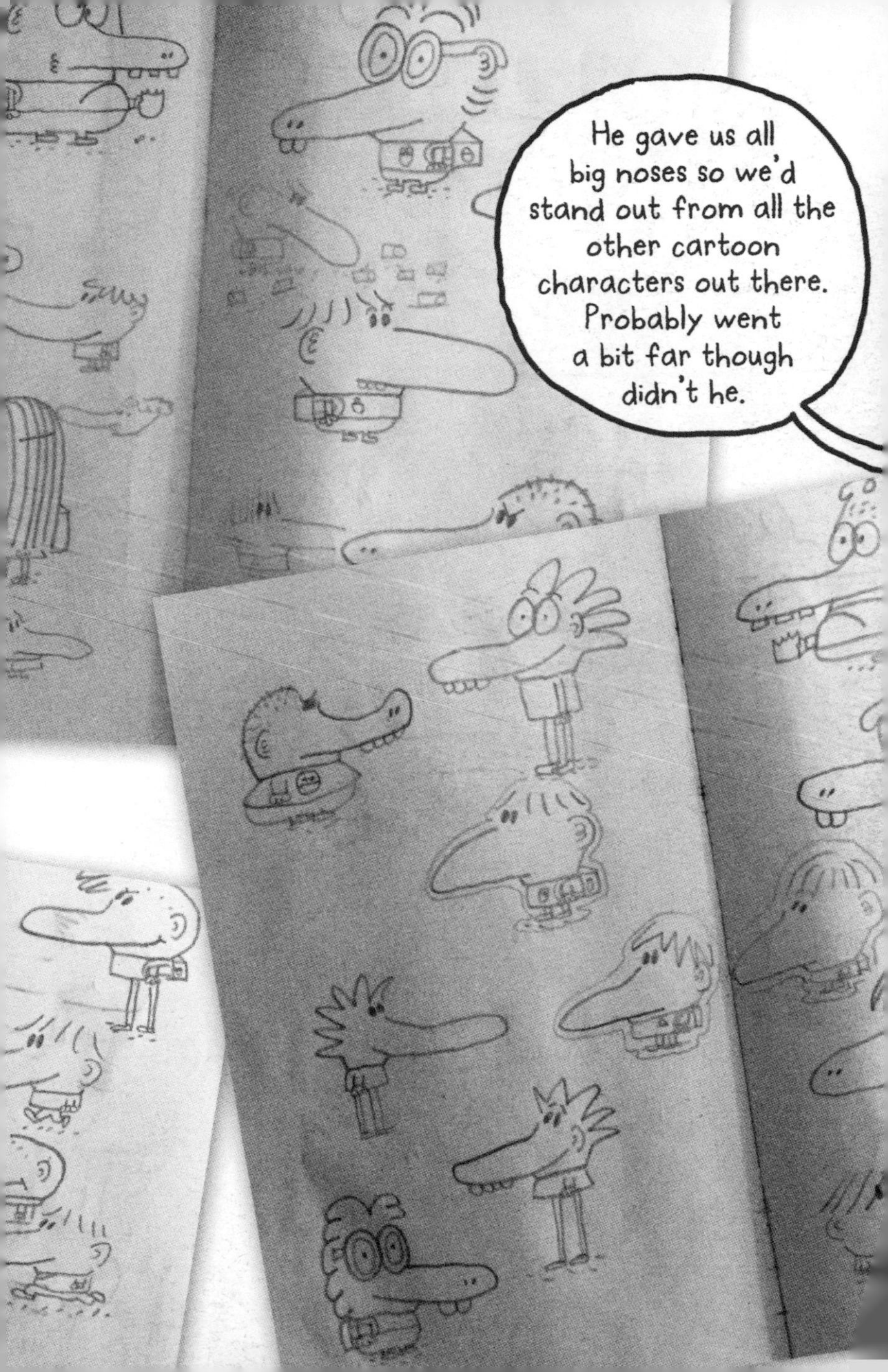
He gave us all big noses so we'd stand out from all the other cartoon characters out there. Probably went a bit far though didn't he.

Design your own Fronkle

When my spellchecker Jim Smith was my age, he had a keeeeel collection of soft drink cans from all over the world. That's why he invented the drink 'Fronkle' and put it in my books.

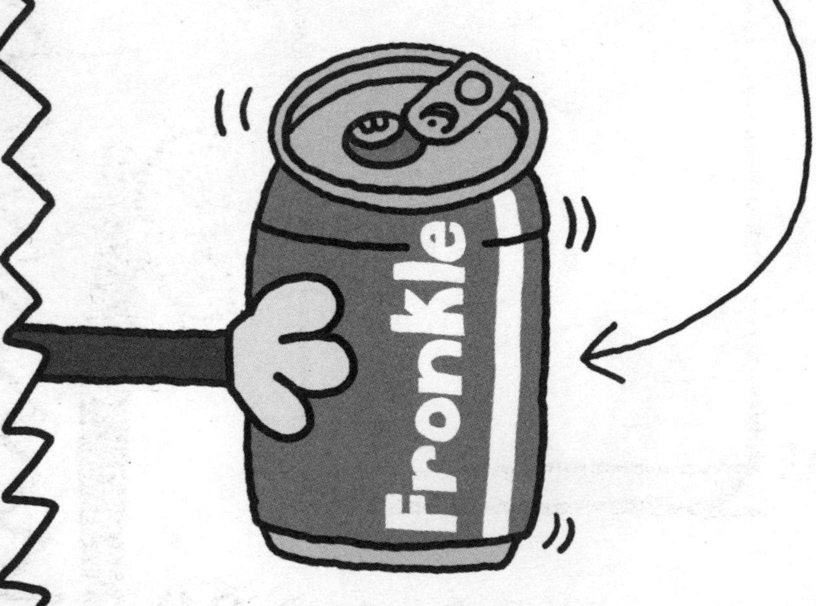
Fronkle

Make up a new flavour of Fronkle and design a can for it!

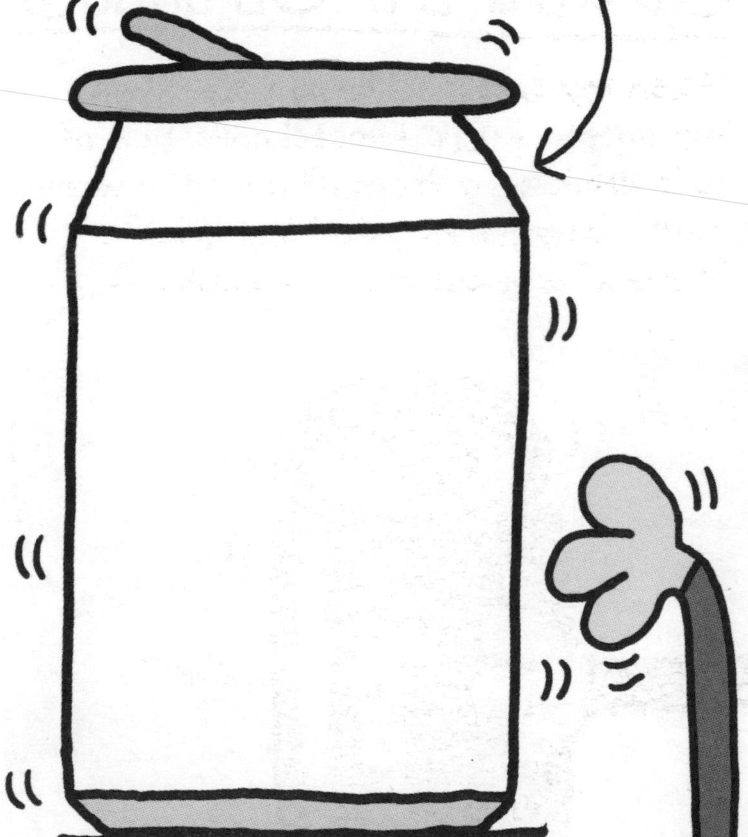

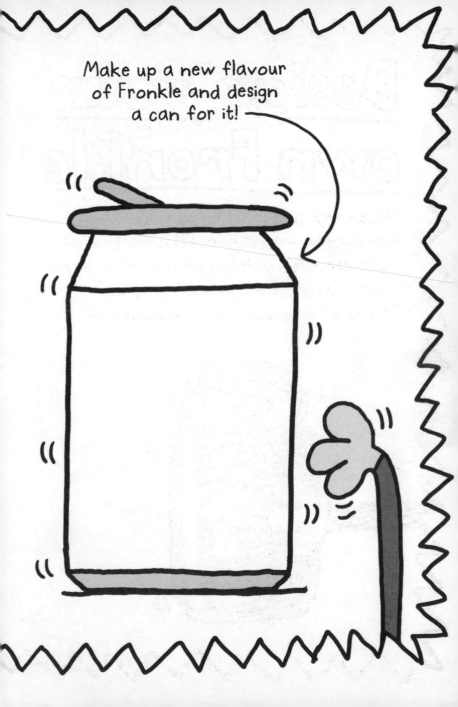

Dear Sharonella

Putting the 'agony' in agony aunt.

DEAR SHARONELLA,

RECENTLY I'VE STARTED CUDDLING MY SPARE PILLOW AT NIGHT. IT'S EVER SO COMFY.

THE PROBLEM IS, I'M WORRIED JOHANN IS JEALOUS. JOHANN IS MY CUDDLY TORTOISE.

WHAT I DO IS, I GO TO SLEEP CUDDLING JOHANN, THEN ONCE HE'S NODDED OFF, I GRAB MY PILLOW AND CUDDLE THAT FOR THE REST OF THE NIGHT.

THEN I WAKE UP JUST BEFORE JOHANN DOES, PUT MY PILLOW BACK IN ITS PLACE, AND START CUDDLING JOHANN AGAIN.

PLEASE CAN YOU HELP ME?

JOHANN

Dear Johann,

Wait, so your name is the same as the tortoise's? That's weird.

Next thing I'm noticing is, IT'S A CUDDLY TOY! They're totes used to being replaced by new ones.

I did the same thing to Sharon my cuddly meerkat. Of course, she never forgave me. Just sits on the shelf giving me the evilz.

Sounds like you've got Johann totes fooled to me. Not really feeling your agony.

That help?

x Sharz x

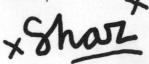

Sharonella's probem pages — first appeared in the Daily Poo newspaper!

BTW, hold this page up to the light.

Oh hi, Loser!

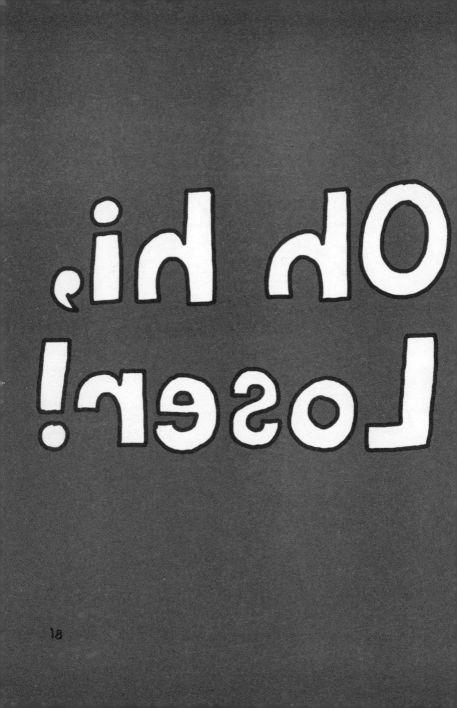

How to draw a Loser

Here's what you'll need:

a pencil

a hand

some eyes

1. always start with eyes – they're the easiest bit

2. add a nose next (make it massive)

(you do it here)

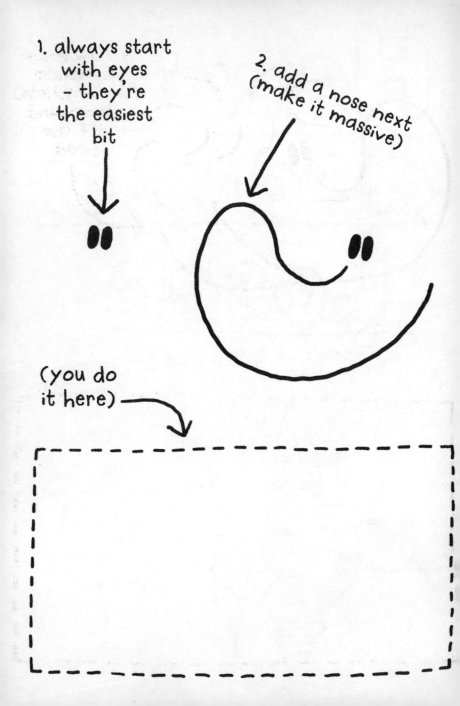

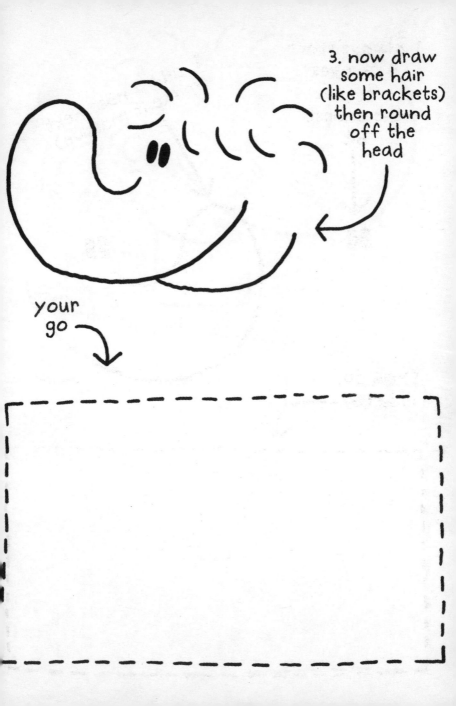

3. now draw
some hair
(like brackets)
then round
off the
head

your
go

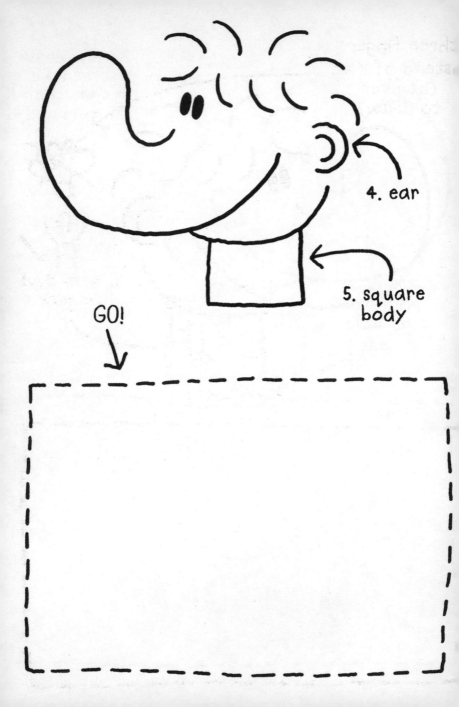

4. ear

5. square body

GO!

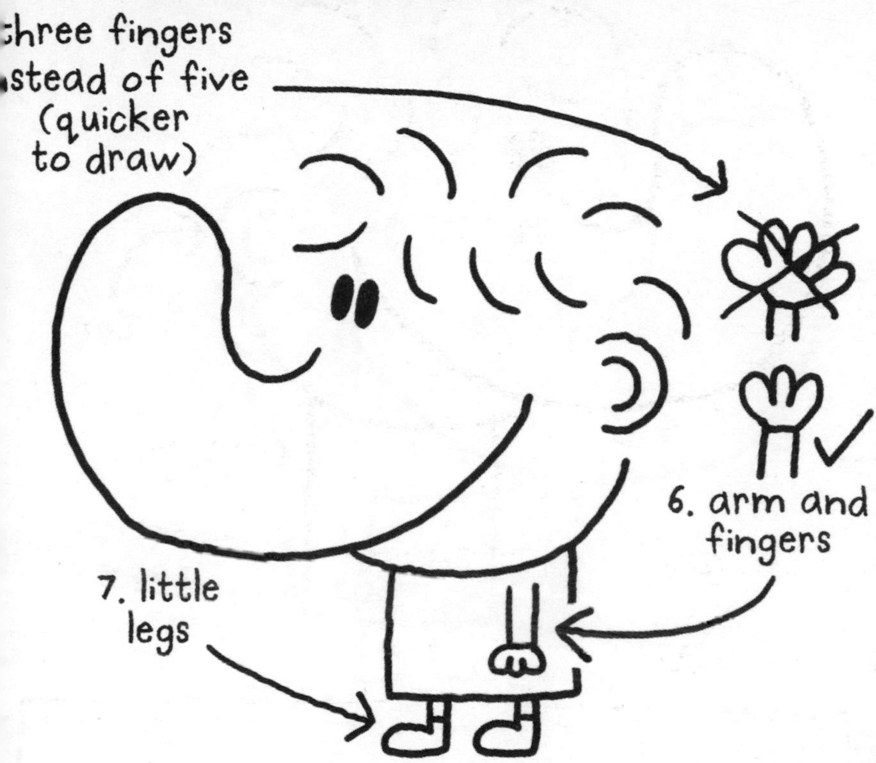
hree fingers
stead of five
(quicker
to draw)
6. arm and
fingers
7. little
legs

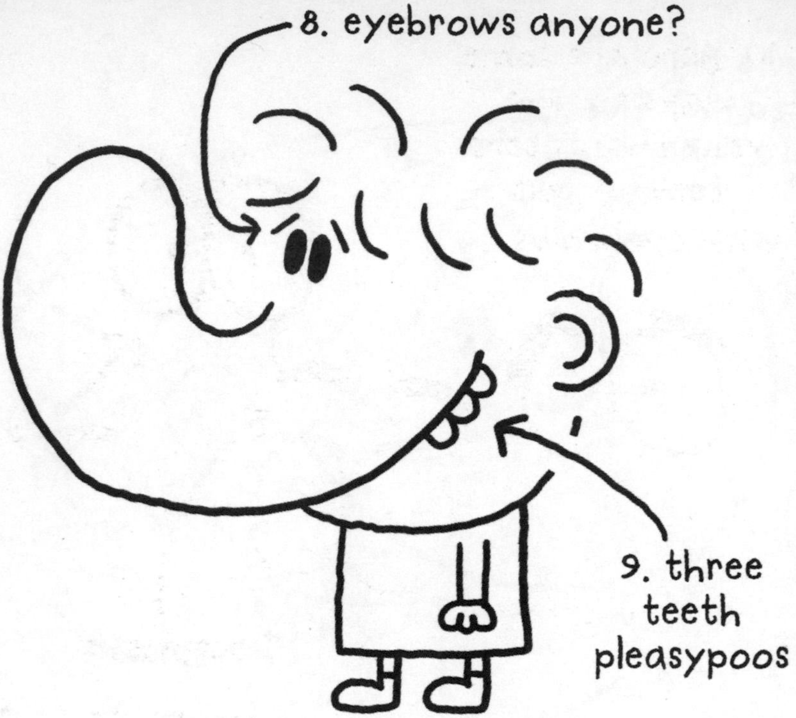
8. eyebrows anyone?
9. three teeth pleasypoos

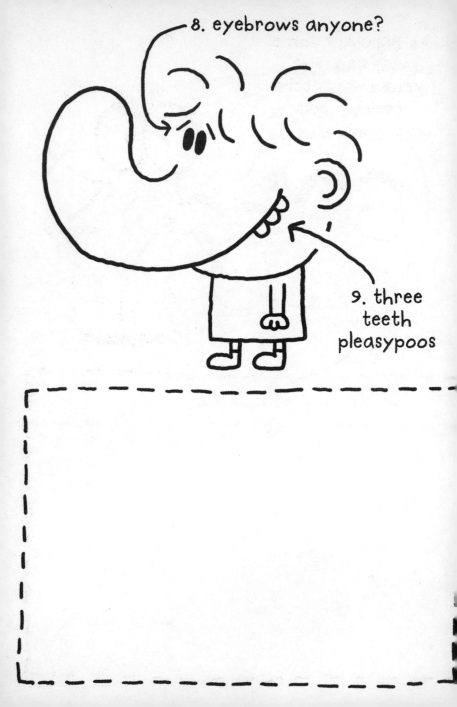

10. here are some ways to give your characters feeling, just with eyebrows. . .

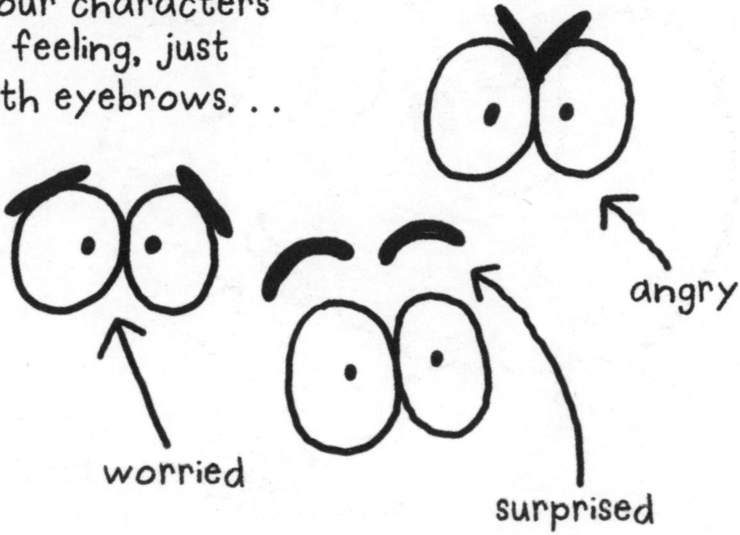
angry
worried
surprised

now get a mirror
and draw yourself!

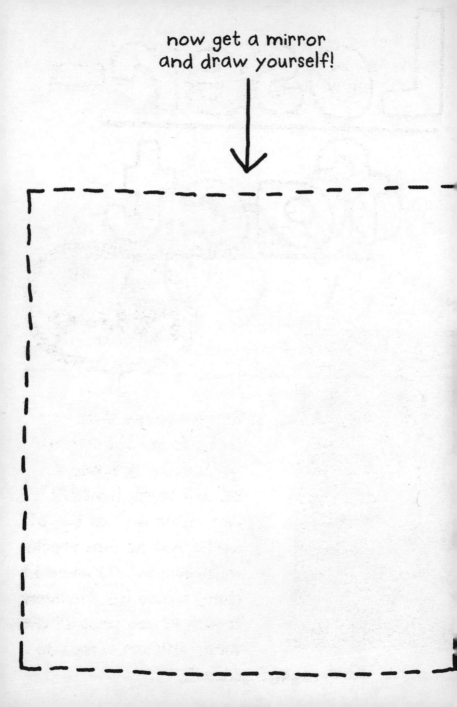

Loser-fact No. 1

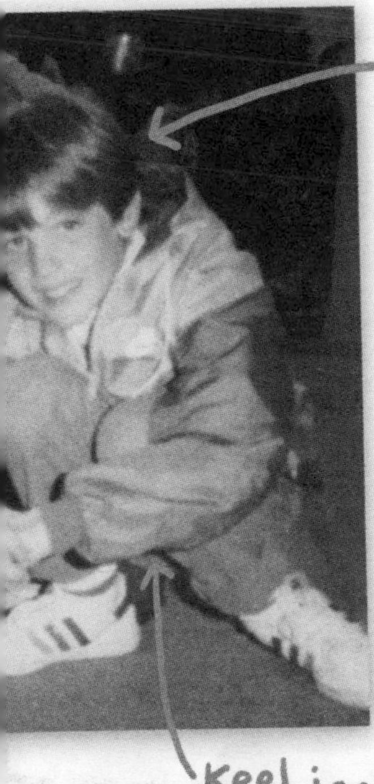
uess who this is? (see page 36)
Jim aged 10
Keel jacket

Did you know that I (me), Barry Loser, am (is) actukeely based on Jim Smith himself? Jim's nose isn't as big, of keelse, but he was pretty much like me (I) when he (him) was a kid. He even treads in dog poos all the time, just like I (me) do (does)!

Meet the Loser friends!

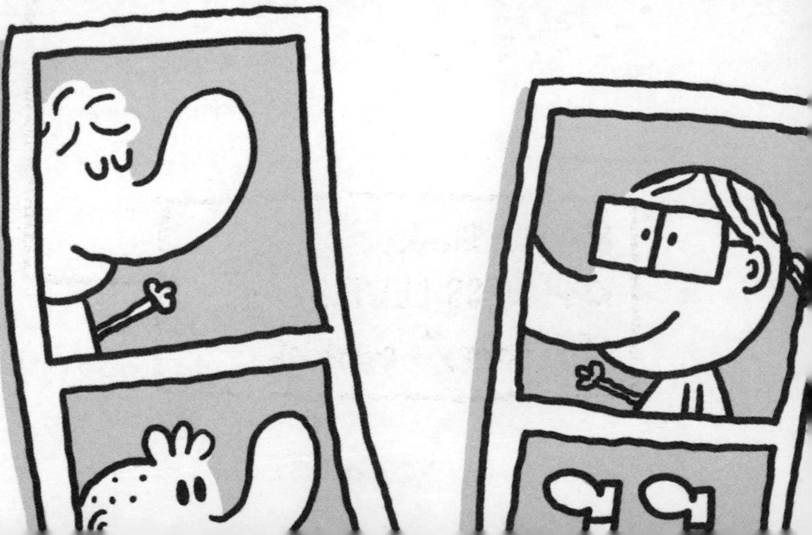

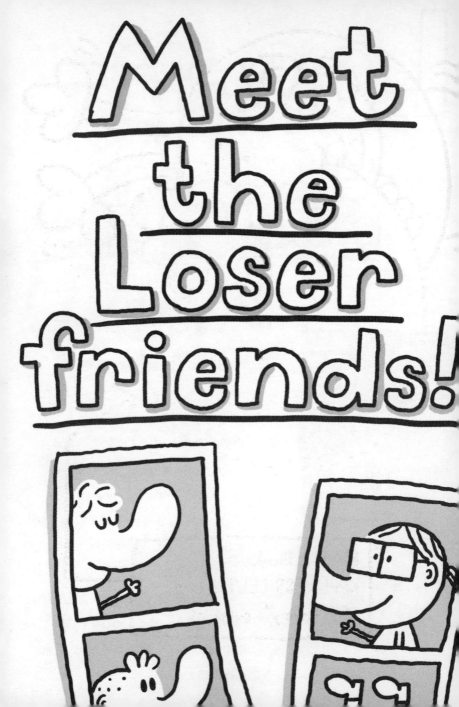

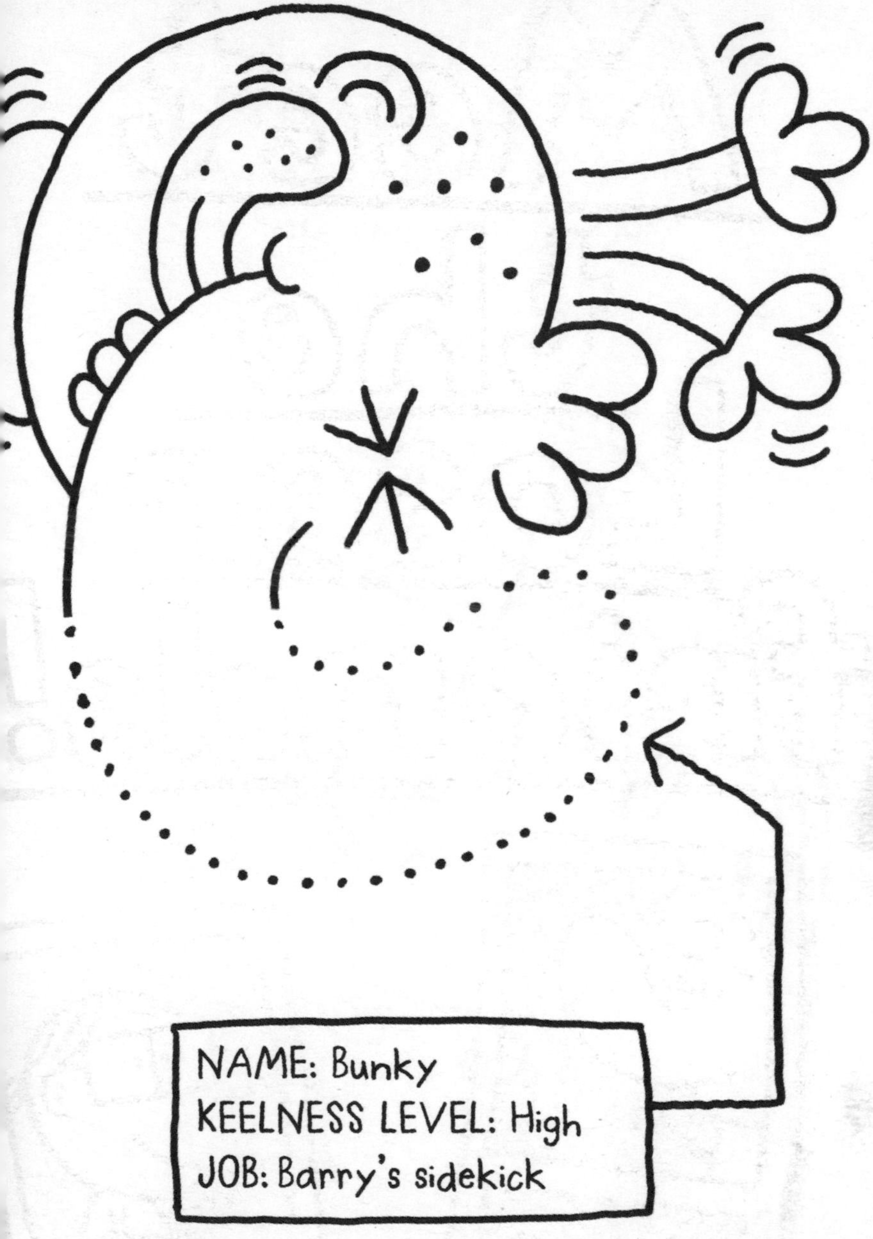

NAME: Bunky
KEELNESS LEVEL: High
JOB: Barry's sidekick

NAME: Nancy Verkenwerken
KEELNESS LEVEL: Quite keel
CAT'S NAME: Gregor Verkenwerken
JOB: Working stuff out for Barry

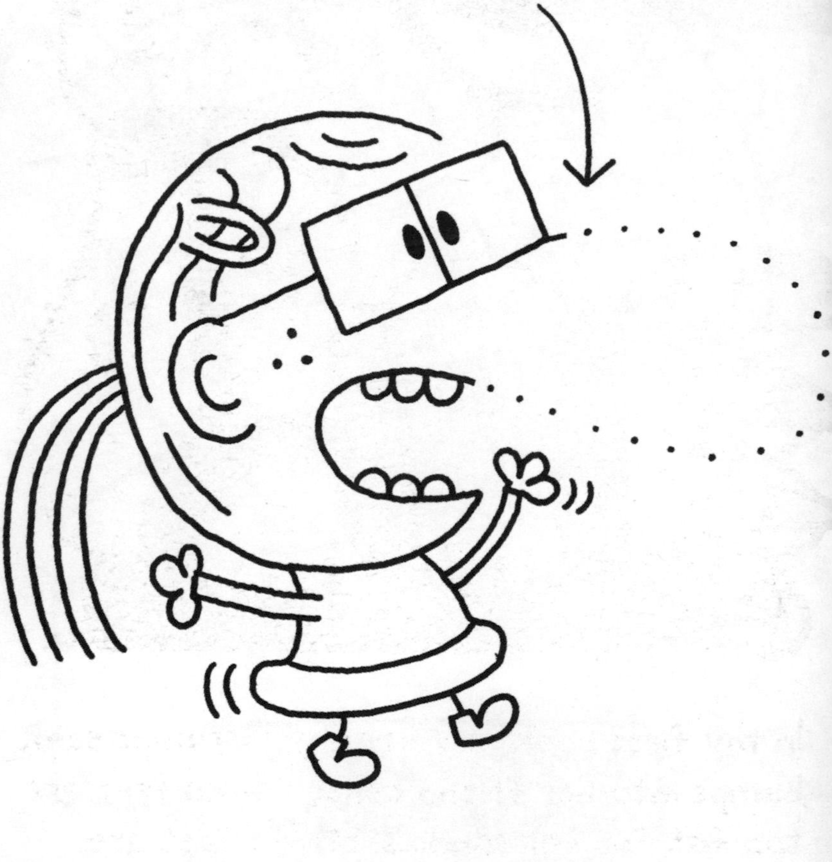

LOSERFACT

②

In my first book, my Granny Harumpadunk bumps into her friend Ethel, whose feet are too fat for her sandals. Ethel's feet are based on Jim Smith's dinner lady's feet from when he was a kid.

DOG POOS!

OR ARE THEY DES'S?

There are lots of dog poos in my books, mostly because dog poos are disgusting and keel. Here are some extra weird ones for you to enjoy.

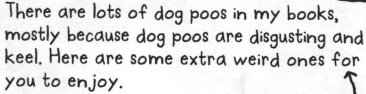

writing made out of dog poo

looks like hand, is actukeely poo

the sideways exclamation mark

tiniest, squarest poo ever

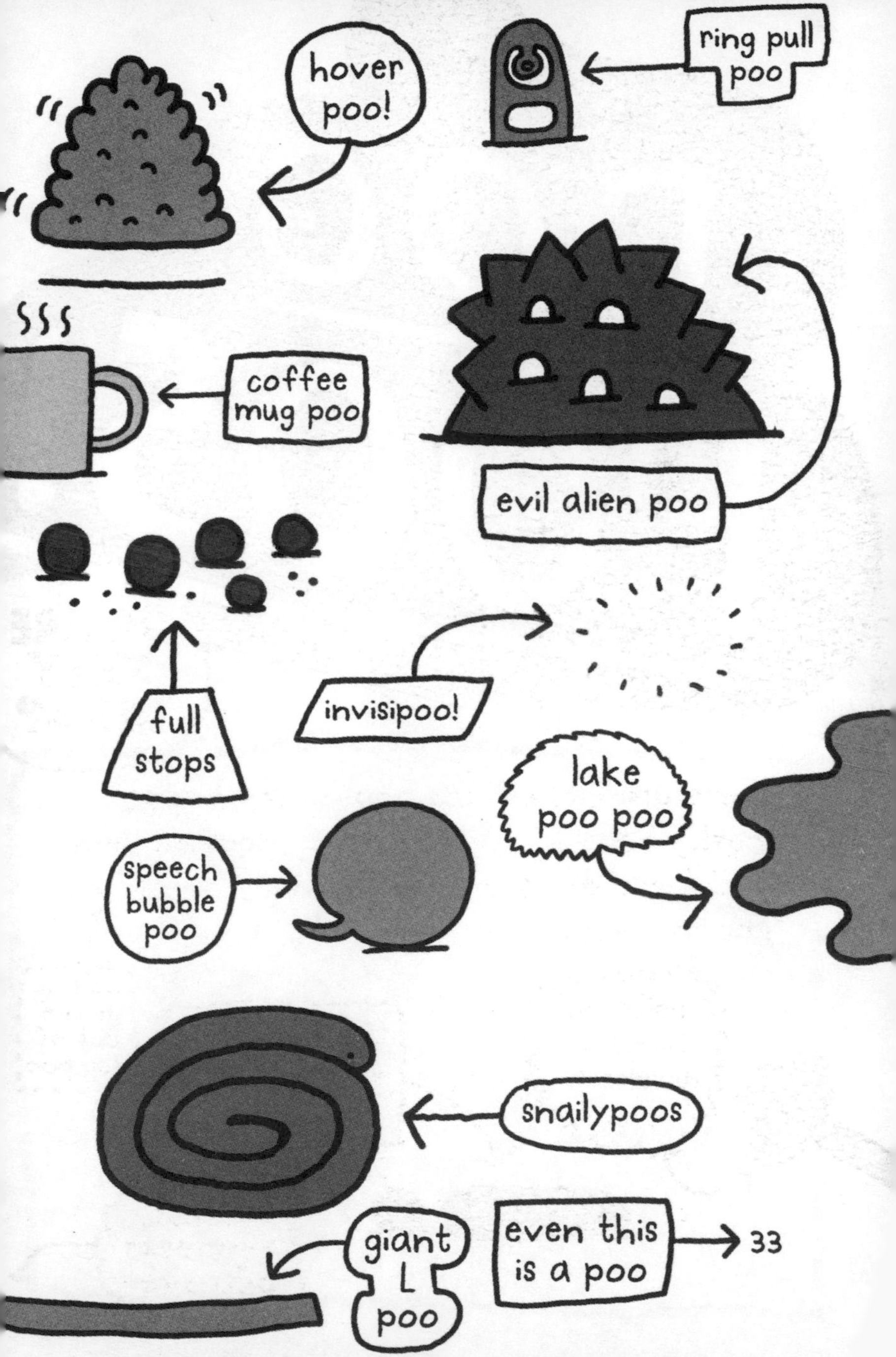
hover poo!
ring pull poo
coffee mug poo
evil alien poo
full stops
invisipoo!
lake poo poo
speech bubble poo
snailypoos
giant L poo
even this is a poo
33

person
stuck
in poo

now do your own!
(drawing, not poo)

ADVERTISEREMENT

BE CAREFUL OF ALL THE DOG POOS EVERYWHERE

Mogden Council

Making Mogden Slightly Better

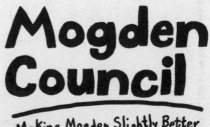

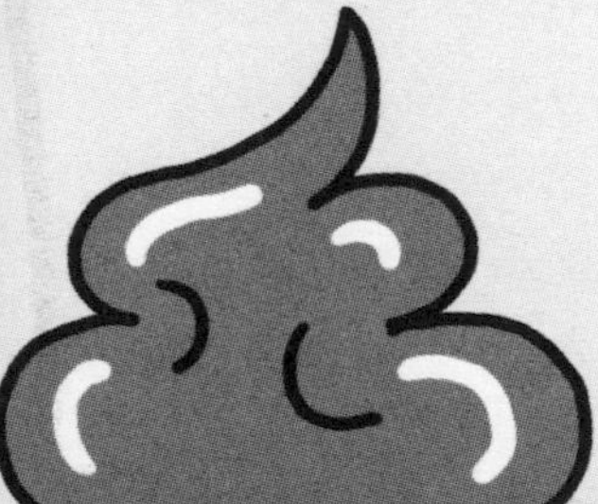

Loserfact 3

My best friend Bunky is based on Jim Smith's best friend when he was a kid.

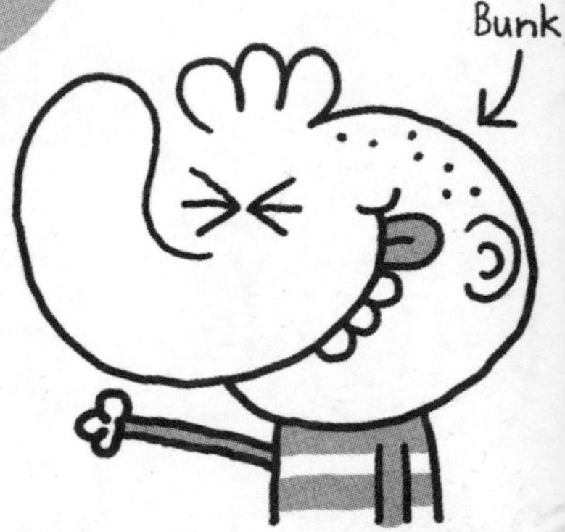
Bunk

He was called Ben, an he was ALWAYS rour Jim's house. During th summer holidays, Ben turned up round Jim' house so early every morning, Jim was usually still in bed.

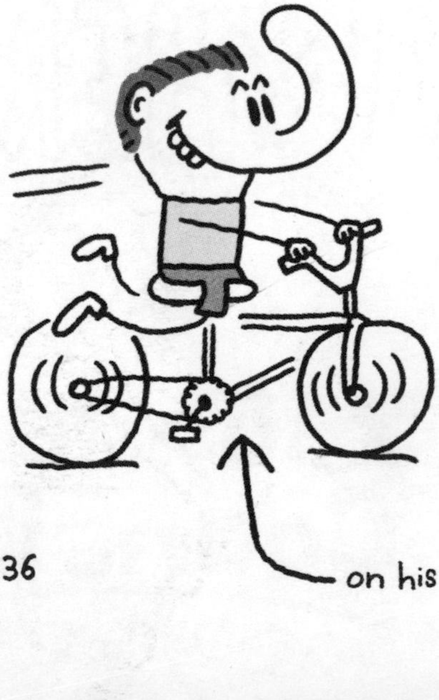
on his way round at 7am

Not that that bothered Ben. Jim's mum would let him in, and he'd make himself at home, watching TV and having a spot of breakfast.

When Jim finally got up and came downstairs, he'd get all annoyed to find Ben sitting on his sofa, living JIM'S life. So he'd send him home.

Jim would calm down after about twenty minutes and call Ben up, ordering him to come back round to play. Which is sort of how I act with Bunky in my books.

1980s phone

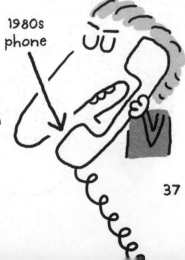

37

Meet the School Losers!

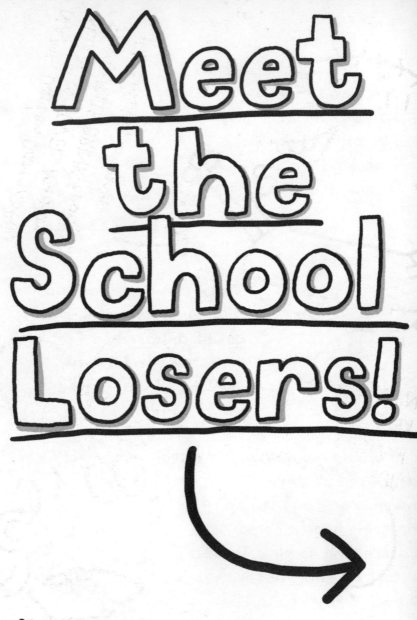

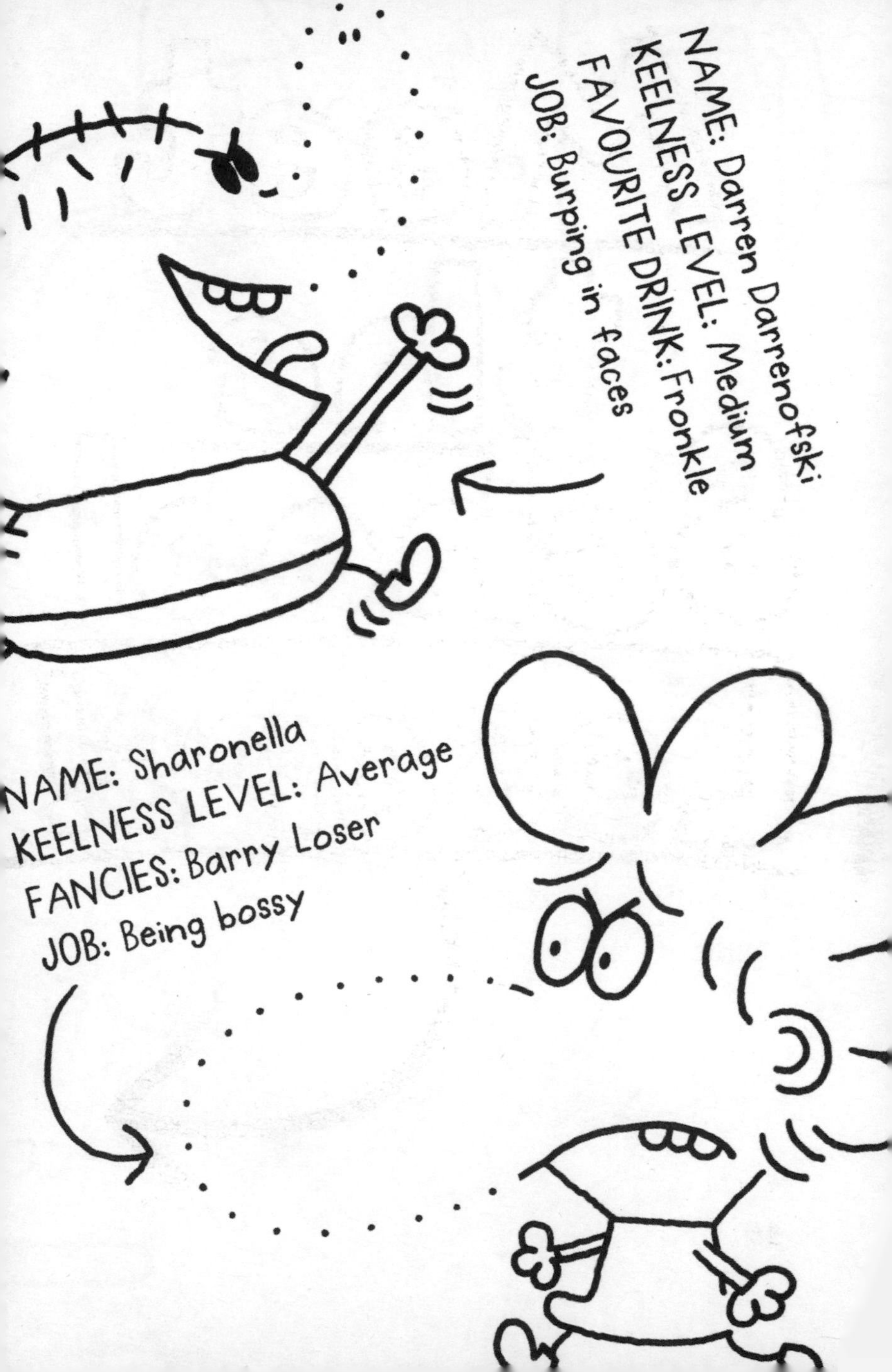
NAME: Darren Darrenofski
KEELNESS LEVEL: Medium
FAVOURITE DRINK: Fronkle
JOB: Burping in faces
NAME: Sharonella
KEELNESS LEVEL: Average
FANCIES: Barry Loser
JOB: Being bossy

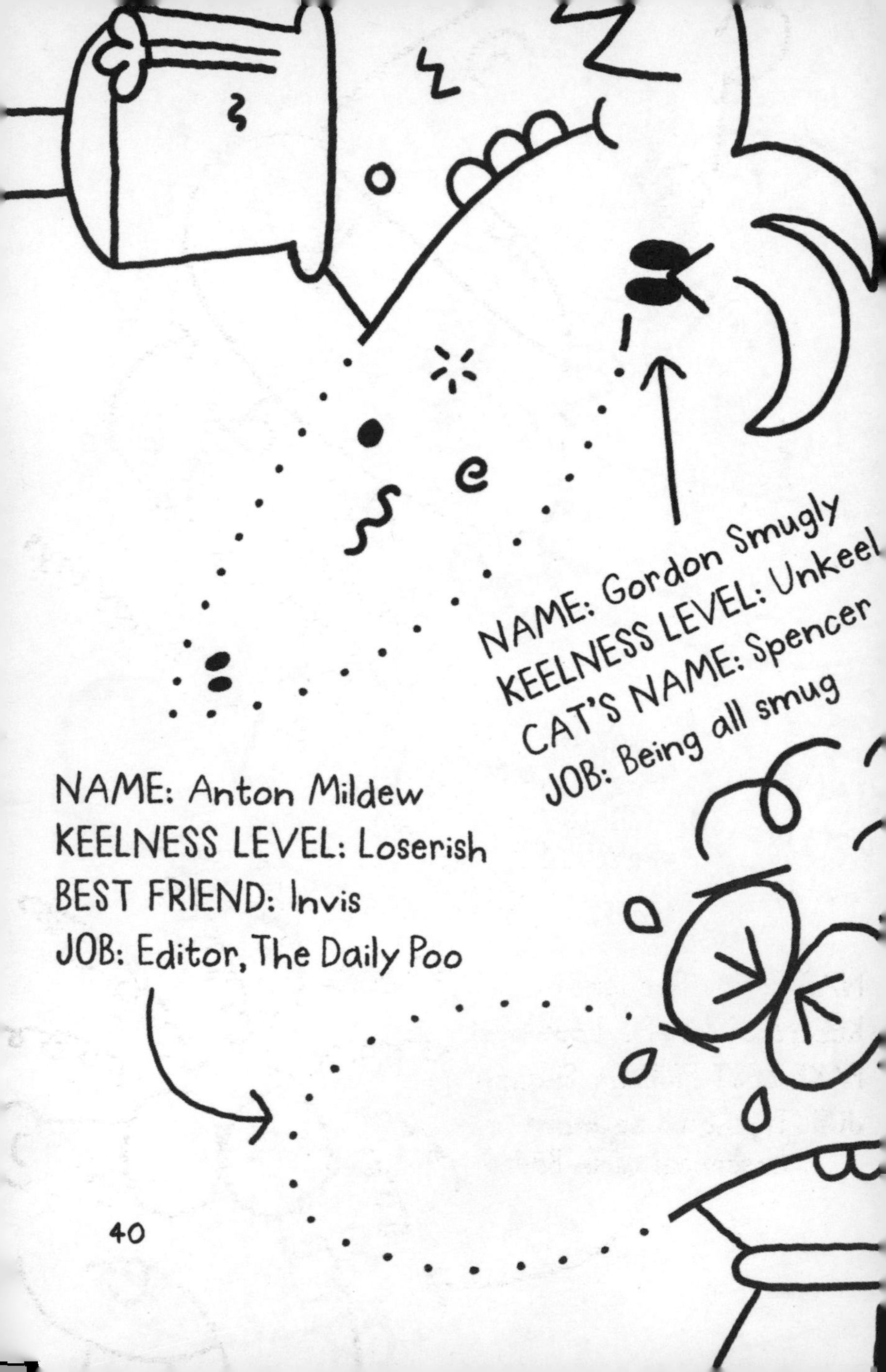
NAME: Gordon Smugly
KEELNESS LEVEL: Unkeel
CAT'S NAME: Spencer
JOB: Being all smug
NAME: Anton Mildew
KEELNESS LEVEL: Loserish
BEST FRIEND: Invis
JOB: Editor, The Daily Poo

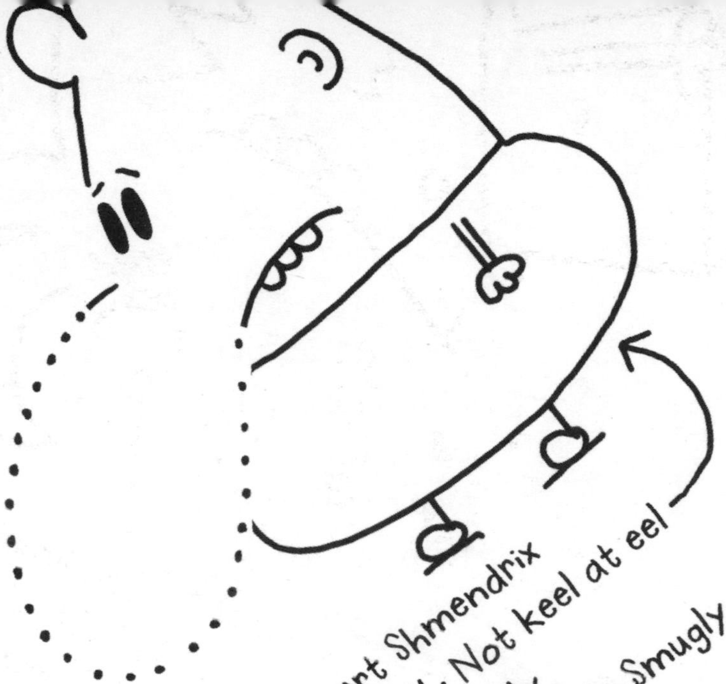

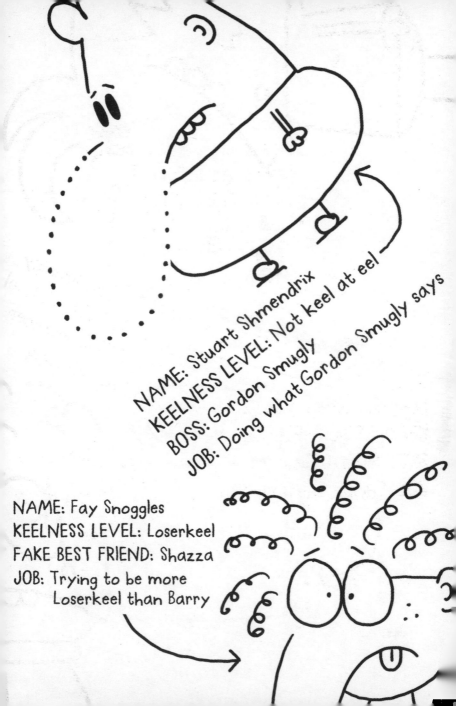

NAME: Stuart Shmendrix
KEELNESS LEVEL: Not keel at eel
BOSS: Gordon Smugly
JOB: Doing what Gordon Smugly says

NAME: Fay Snoggles
KEELNESS LEVEL: Loserkeel
FAKE BEST FRIEND: Shazza
JOB: Trying to be more Loserkeel than Barry

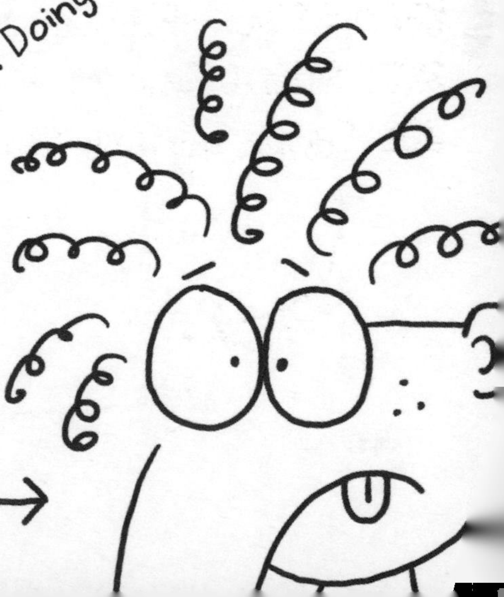

Anton Mildew from my class is the editor of our school newspaper, The Daily Poo. Here's a few pages from one of them!

(printed on recycled toilet paper)

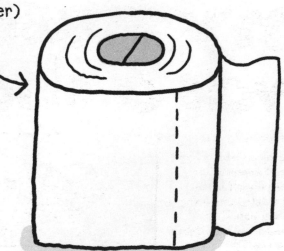

The Daily Poo

Edited by Anton Mildew

Everyone thought my nose was a shark

by A. Person

I was lying on my back in Mogden Swimming Pool enjoying myself when people started screaming. I spose my nose IS a bit grey and triangle-ly. Didn't think it was THAT bad though.

Didn't they see my hands and feet?

Ring pull collection stolen

by Darren Darrenofski

Someone's stolen all my ring pulls! I had them in my pockets. My mum sewed them into my jacket specially (the pockets, not the ring pulls). There were like eight million of them (ring pulls, not pockets).

Now I've got to start again. *Opens can of Fronkle*

Wait a minute, I've just found them all in another pocket. Panic over.

Me showing someone one of my ring pulls

The poo poo

Ah, the poo poo!

So smelly they named it twice

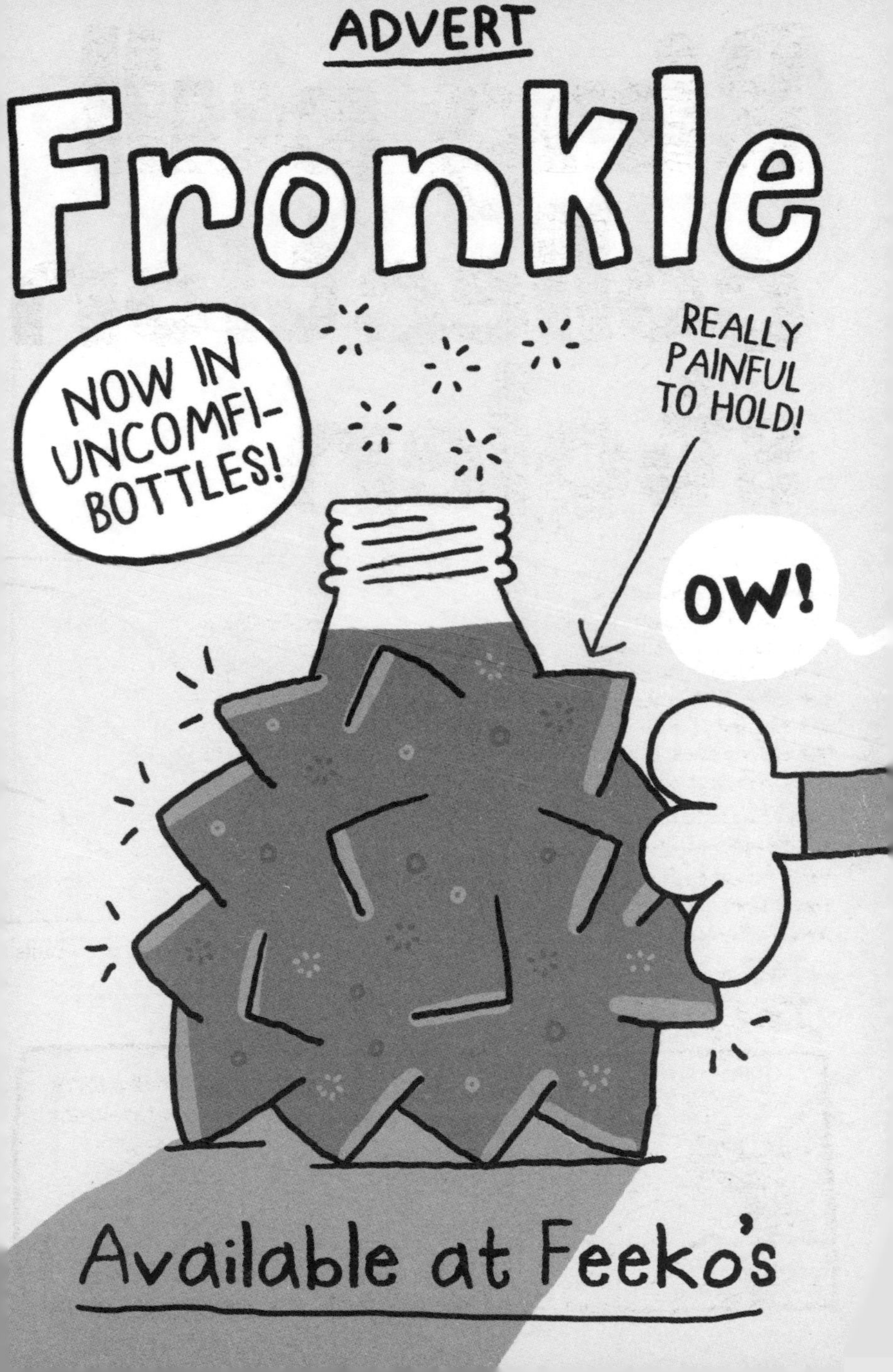
ADVERT
Fronkle
NOW IN UNCOMFI-BOTTLES!
REALLY PAINFUL TO HOLD!
OW!
Available at Feeko's

Man tiptoes round world

by Fay Snoggles

A man has traversed the globe after dropping his glove in the street.

'I couldn't be bothered to turn and pick it up, so I walked all the way round the world for it instead,' chortled Brian Davies, who tiptoed the entire thing so as not to wake anyone up.

Amazingly, the glove was still where he'd dropped it, despite the trip taking nineteen years.

'I could've done with it on the walk!' laughed Brian, whose left hand froze and then fell off during the expedition.

glove
directon of walk
Brian

Photo by Gaspar Pink

Thinks

I've just discovered thought bubbles!
Now I can think what I want about these losers!
I saw that

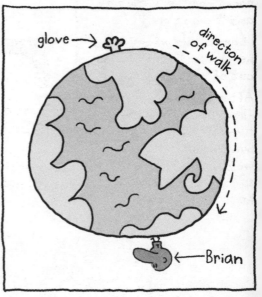

Fly won't fly off

Barry Loser on the scene

There's this really annoying fly that's been in my room for the whole day and it won't go.

I opened the window and he just sat there looking out of it at the view.

After that he got up and flew round my room twenty times then started bumping into the bit of window that wasn't open, so I opened that too and he sat down again.

After that he flew round my room another eight million times and now he's on my shelf eating an old dried-up droplet of Fronkle.

Cola Flavour

Not Birds

Some woman counts every brick in town

by Anton Mildew

A Mogden lady has spent her whole life counting how many bricks there are in the whole town. 'I'm up to eight trillion, seven hundred and twenty-three billion, five hundred and forty-seven million, six hundred and ninety-two thousand, one hundred and thirteen. Or is it fourteen? Oh, I've lost count, I'd better start again!' she says ripping up a really thick notepad. 'One, two, three . . .' she said, as I walked off.

Some of those bricks I was just talking about.

ADVERTYWERT

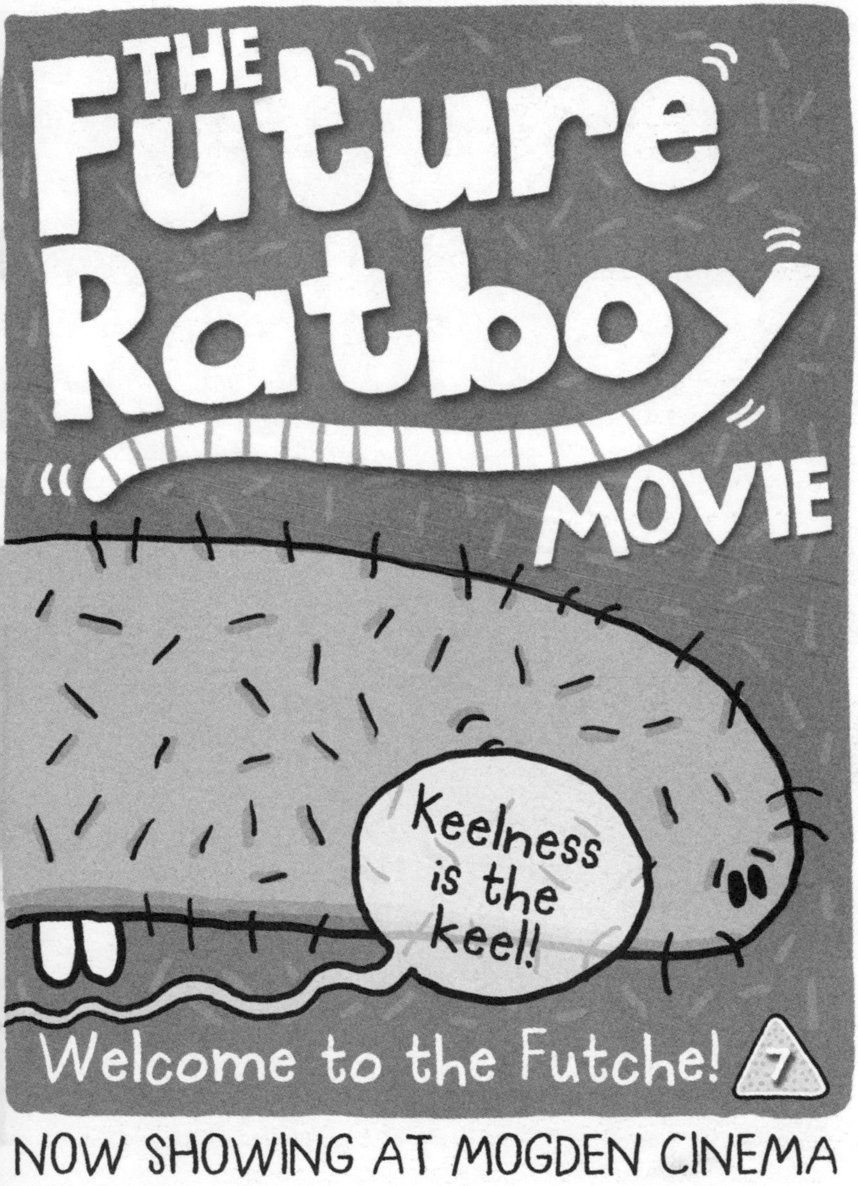
THE Future Ratboy MOVIE
Keelness is the keel!
Welcome to the Futche!
7

NOW SHOWING AT MOGDEN CINEMA

ADVERTINGTONS

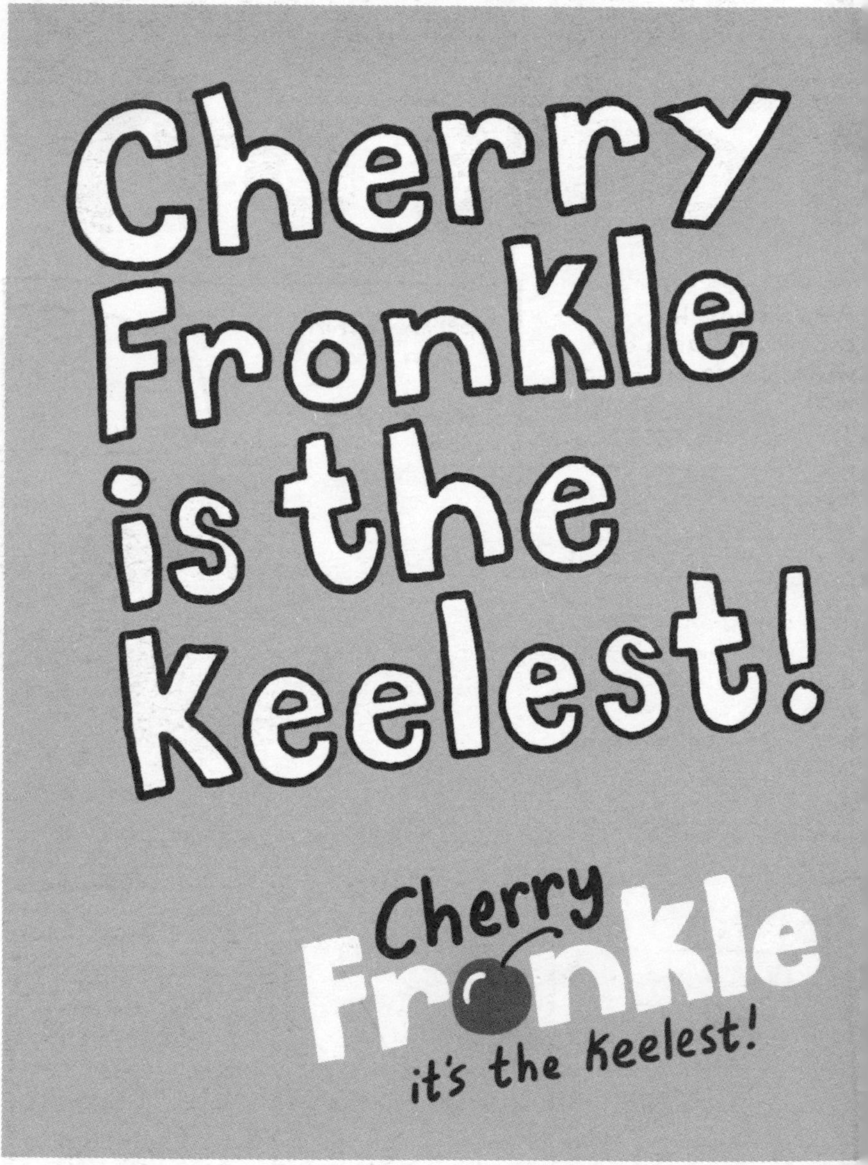
Cherry Fronkle is the Keelest!
Cherry Fronkle
it's the keelest!

Man's nose falls off

Gaspar Pink reports

A man's nose has completely fallen off while he was out for a walk.

The man, who also has no name, was looking in a shop window when he saw his nose start to slip off his face in the reflection.

'It dropped onto the pavement and rolled down a drain,' said the man, in a weird voice, because of his no nose.

'Now all I can smell is drains,' he continued as I walked off, all bored.

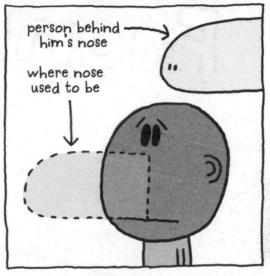

person behind him's nose →

where nose used to be ↓

The man with no name nor nose

Yawn

I caught a yawn from someone in a film the other day

I'm yawning just thinking about it

I'm yawning thinking about you thinking about it!

I'm yawning listening to you two

Design your own paper →

Here's what you've got to come up with:

1. a newspaper name
2. a headline for your story
3. then write the story
4. and draw a photo for it

NEWSPAPER

Headline

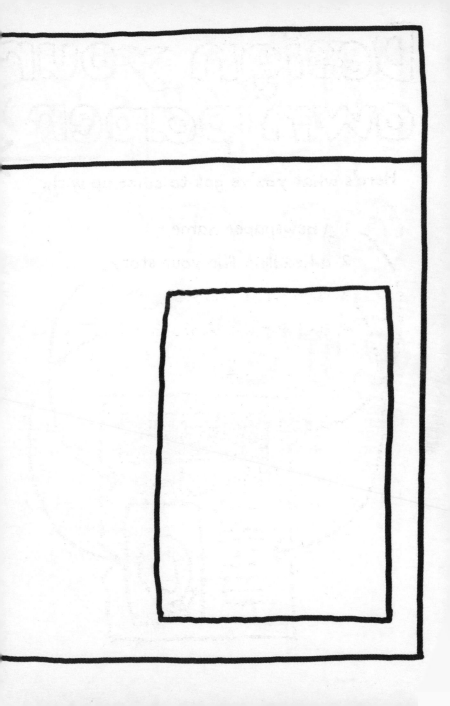

How to draw a drawer

Everyone knows drawers are the hardest thing to draw in the whole wide world. But don't worry, I'm about to teach you how to draw a drawer in three easy steps. By the way, steps are the second-hardest thing to draw in the whole wide world.

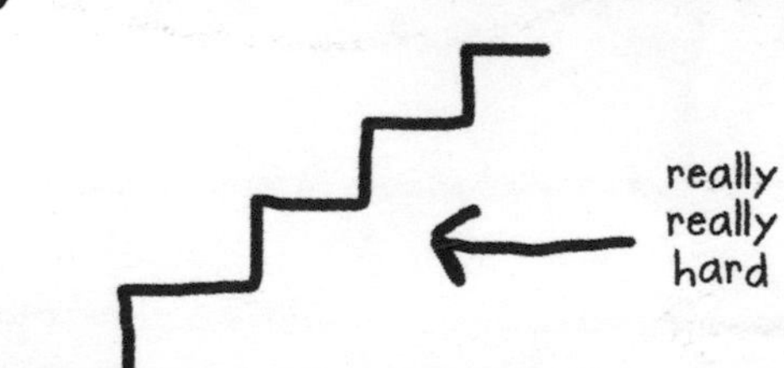
really
really
hard

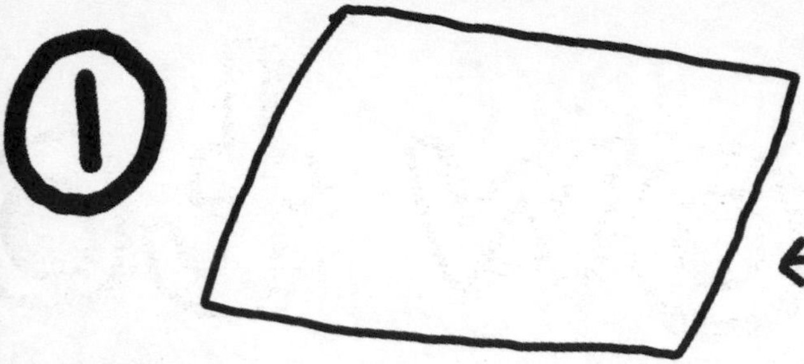

Draw a squidged square (which is actukeely called a 'paralellogram').

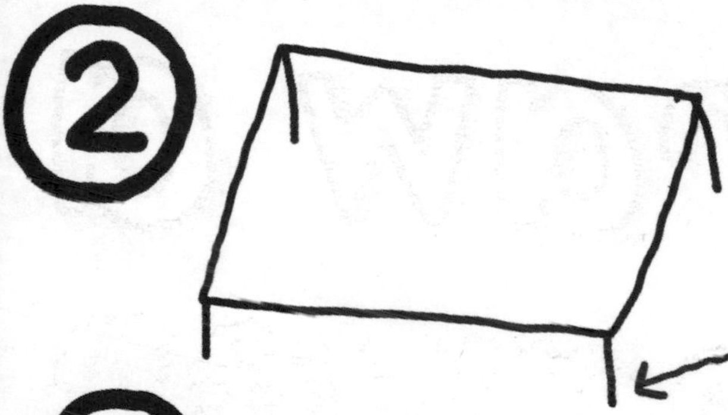

Now add little legs to the squidged square. By the way, you now know how to draw a glass-topped table.

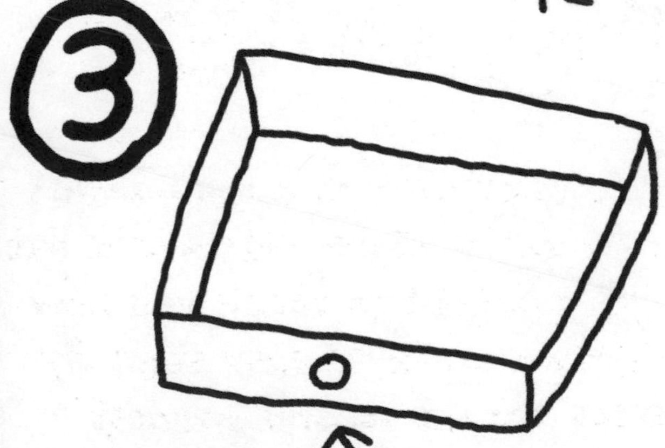

Join up the ends of the little legs and draw a circle for the drawer's handle. I have now realised that drawing a drawer is actukeely one of the easiest things to draw in the world.

Draw your own drawer down here. Not that anyone's gonna be impressed cos it's SO easy.

More Sketches

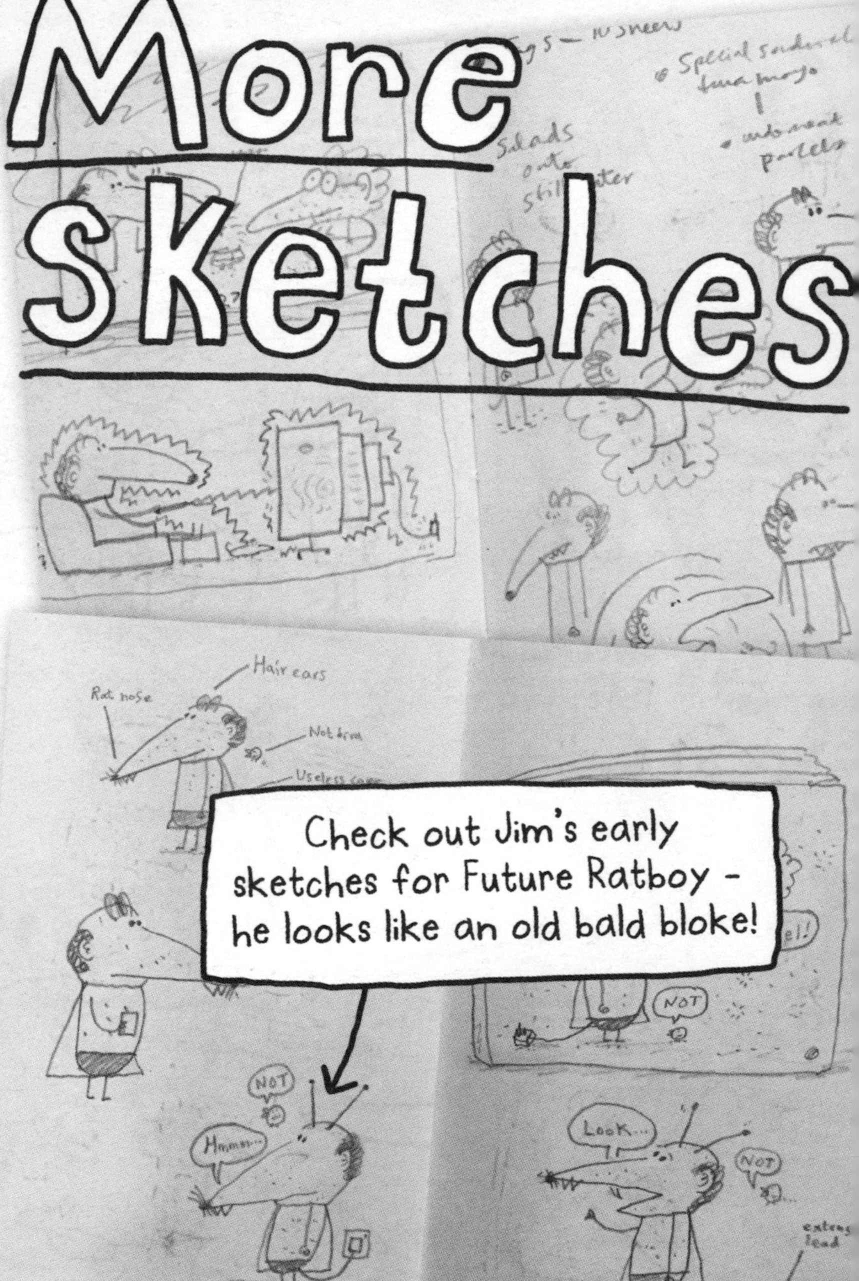

Hair ears
Rat nose
NOT
NOT
Look...
NOT

Check out Jim's early sketches for Future Ratboy – he looks like an old bald bloke!

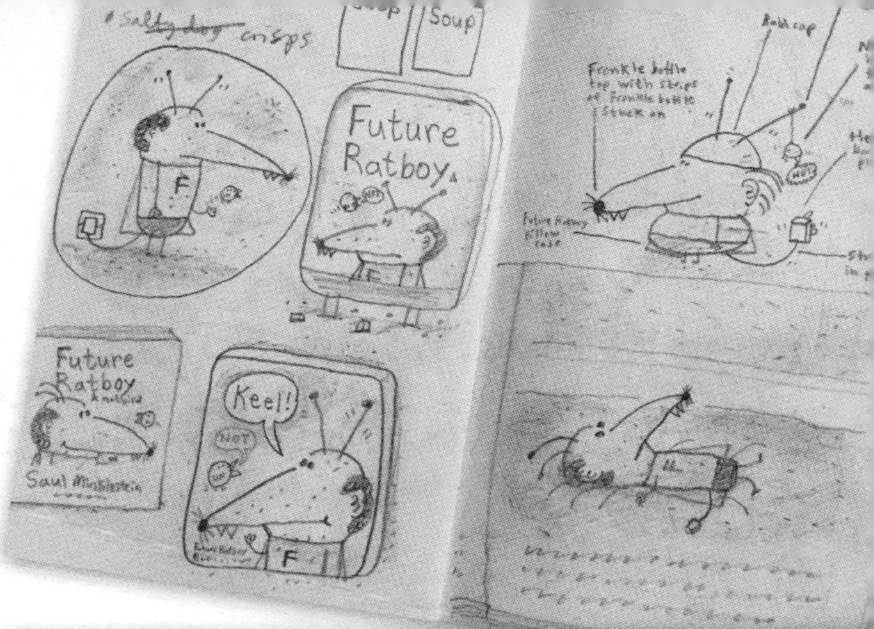
Soup
Future Ratboy
Future Ratboy
Saul Minklestein
Keel!
NOT

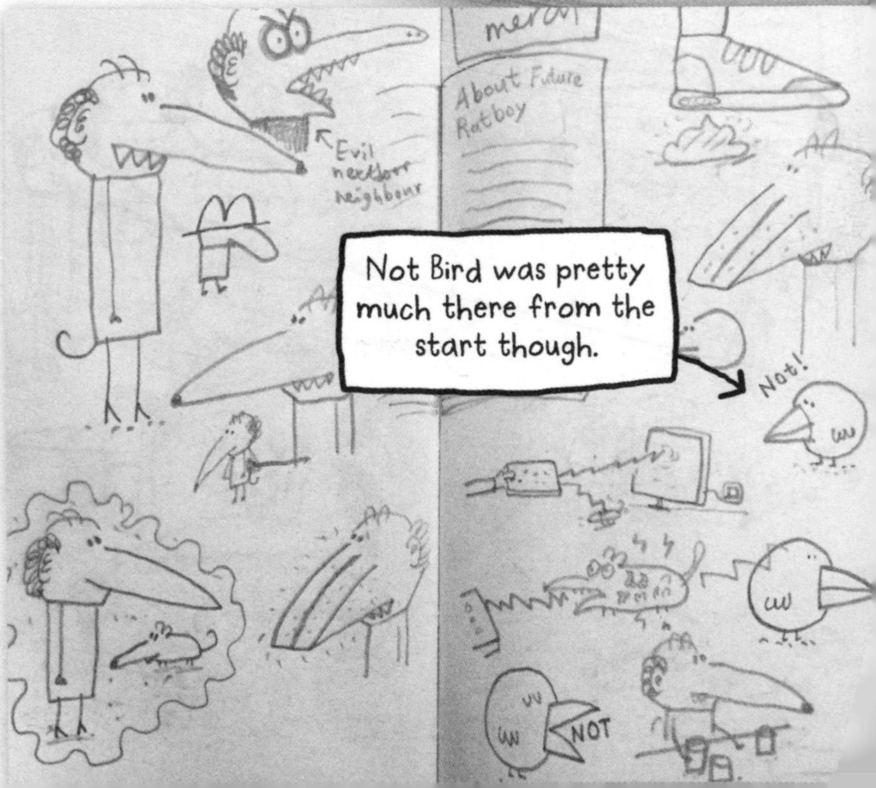
Evil
neighbour
About Future Ratboy
Not Bird was pretty much there from the start though.
Not!
NOT

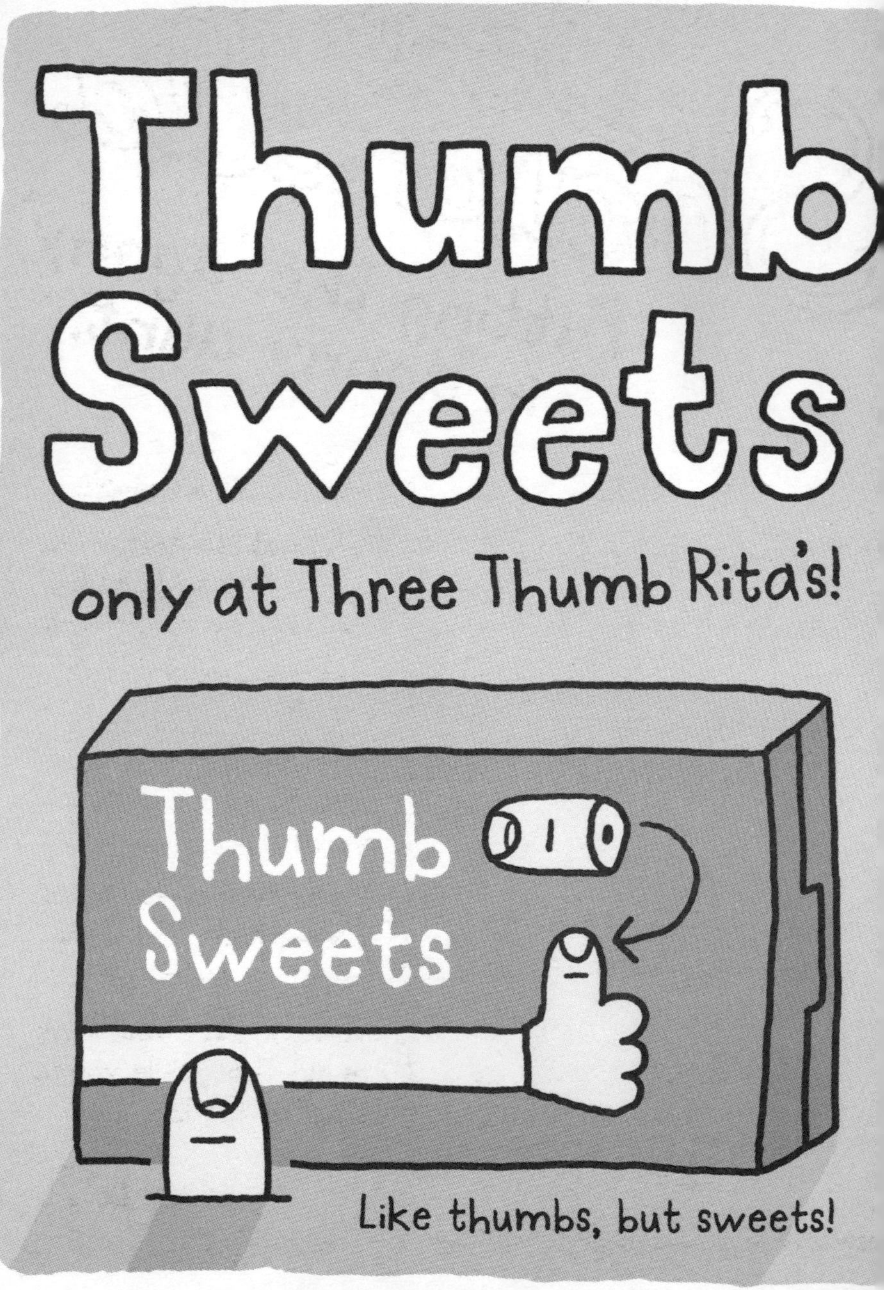
Thumb Sweets
only at Three Thumb Rita's!
Thumb Sweets
Like thumbs, but sweets!

Dear Sharonella

Putting the 'agony' in agony aunt.

dear Shaz, HELP!! I'm stuck in the loo! that's why this is on loo paper. lucky I had a pen wasn't it!

Yeah, so anyway... about being locked in the toilet. any advice?

Yours,

too embarrassed to say who i am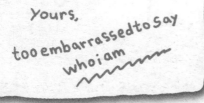

Dear whoeveryouare,

I note at the end of your note you wrote 'yours' just before your name.

Does that mean you are mine?

If so, this is more my problem than it is yours.

Which makes you a bit selfish, moaning to me about it, doesn't it.

So why don't you think about that while you're stuck in the loo.

SHAZ

LOSERISH JOKES!

-APOLOGIES IN ADVANCE

Who is the keelest person in the world?
-Barry Loser!

Which Barry is asleep?
-Barry Snoozer

Hey, these are hilarious!

WHICH BARRY NEVER LIES?
-BARRY TRUESER

Which Barry is feeling a bit sad?
-Barry Blueser

HA HA HA HA HA!

Which Barry lives in a toilet?
-BARRY POOSER!

Which Barry used to be really small?
-Barry GREWSER

Which Barry went on holiday on Smeldorian Airlines?
-Barry Flewser

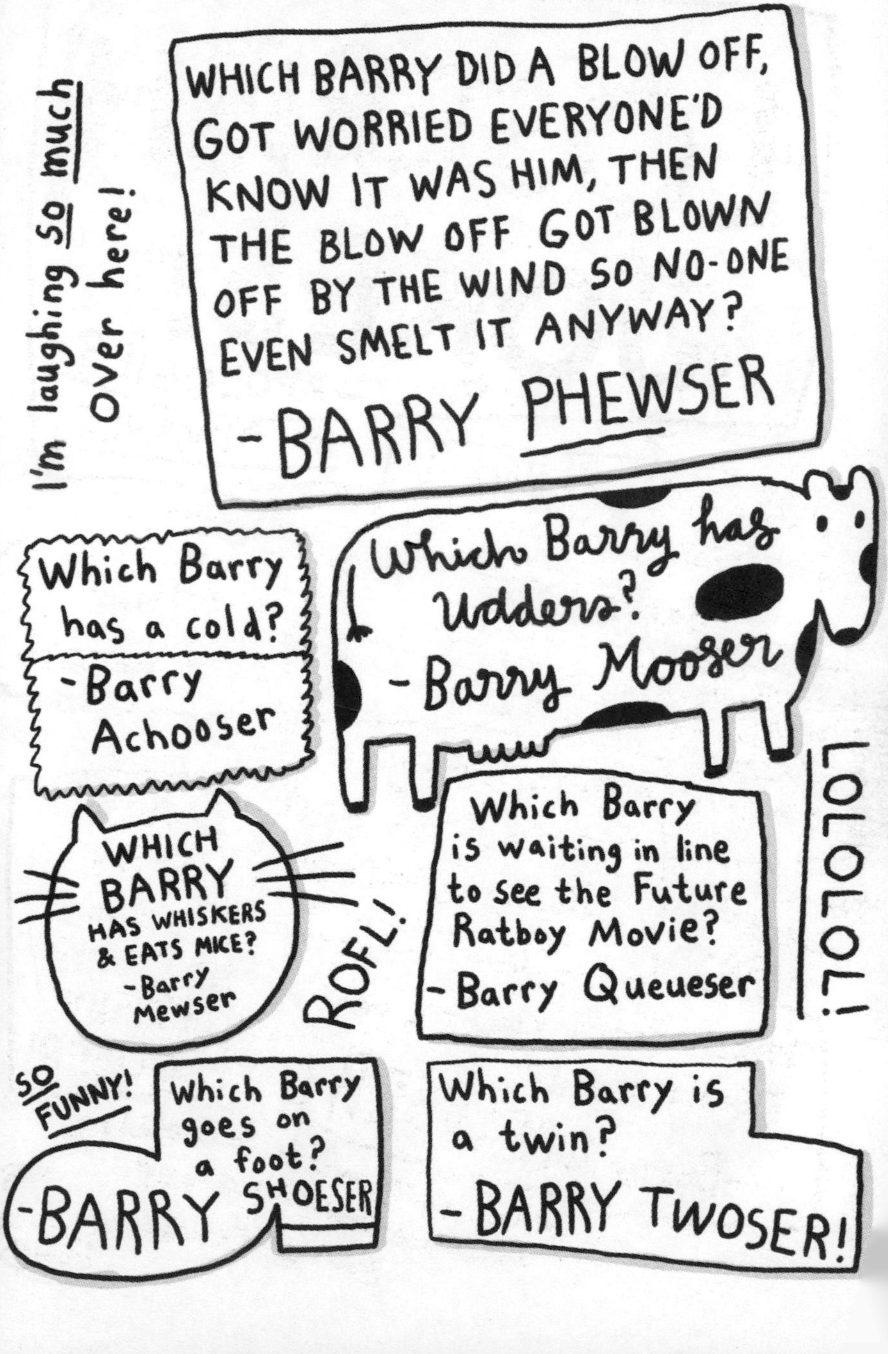
I'm laughing so much over here!
WHICH BARRY DID A BLOW OFF, GOT WORRIED EVERYONE'D KNOW IT WAS HIM, THEN THE BLOW OFF GOT BLOWN OFF BY THE WIND SO NO-ONE EVEN SMELT IT ANYWAY?
-BARRY PHEWSER
Which Barry has a cold?
-Barry Achooser
Which Barry has udders?
-Barry Mooser
WHICH BARRY HAS WHISKERS & EATS MICE?
-Barry Mewser
ROFL!
Which Barry is waiting in line to see the Future Ratboy Movie?
-Barry Queueser
LOLOLOL!
SO FUNNY!
Which Barry goes on a foot?
-BARRY SHOESER
Which Barry is a twin?
-BARRY TWOSER!

FOOD DRAWINGS!

I like food. I like drawing.
I like food drawing!

MINI FACTOID: Did you know, cookies HATE page numbers (AND the number sixty-two).

CAUTION: THIS HAS NOTHING TO DO WITH MY BOOKS REALLY

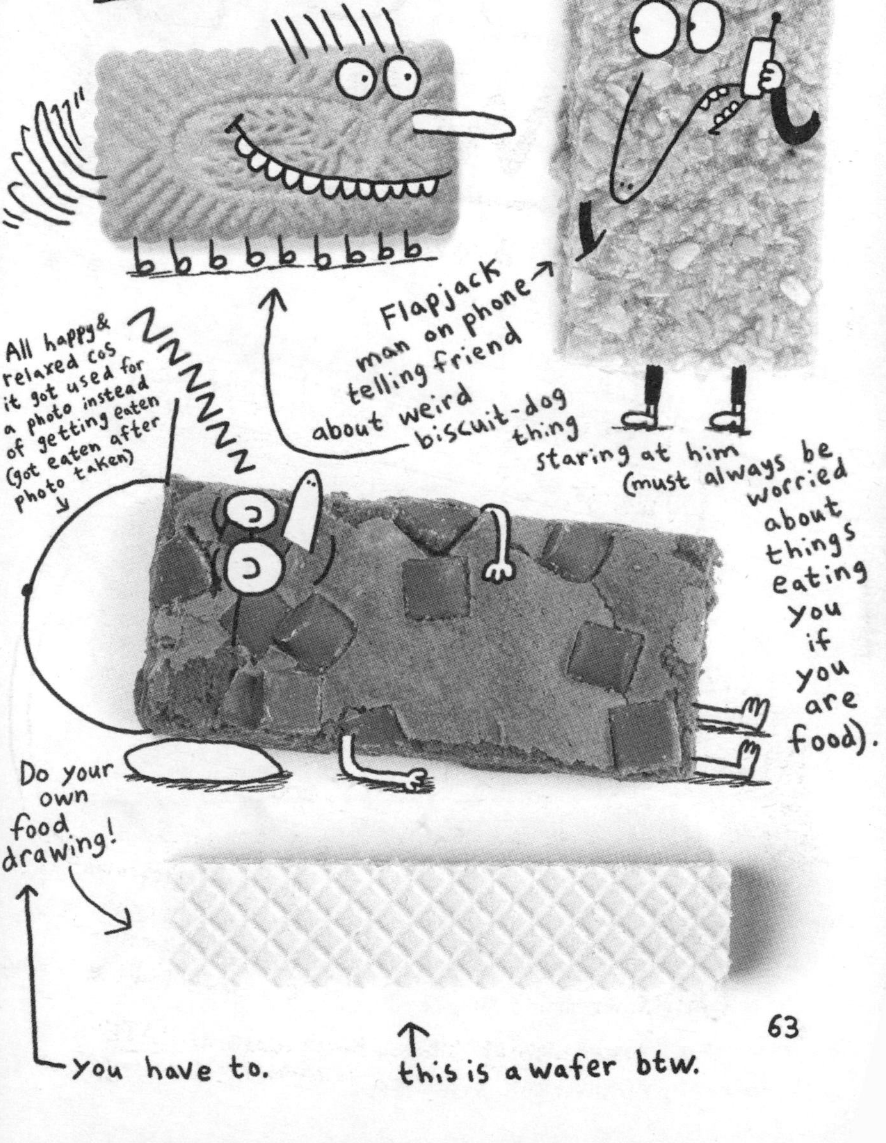

bbbbbbbbb
Flapjack man on phone telling friend about weird biscuit-dog thing staring at him (must always be worried about things eating you if you are food).
All happy & relaxed cos it got used for a photo instead of getting eaten (got eaten after photo taken)
ZZZZZZZ
Do your own food drawing!
you have to.
this is a wafer btw.

What Sort of Loser are you?

What do you want to do when you grow up?

a) Become a billionaire from all my amazekeel inventions
b) Be a billionaire's assistant and follow my boss around like a dog
c) Be a librarian or prime minister
d) Become a famous YouTube star
e) Do a really BORING job in an office

What's your ideal pet?

a) Something keel like a tiger or a monkey butler
b) DOG
c) Something intelligent like a cat or a pig
d) One of them little dogs that fits in your handbag
e) Anything that doesn't mess up the house

What's your FAVE meal?

a) Fish fingers, chips and Passion-Fruit flavour Fronkle
b) Thumb sweets
c) Nuts and leaves
d) Sausages
e) Egg cress sarnies & a mug of disgusting coffee

What's your best Subject at School?

a) I'm pretty good at everything
b) PE
c) Maths
d) Drama
e) I went to school a million years ago

65

Who is your secret crush?

a) Michael J Socks
b) Nancy Verkenwerken
c) Wolf Tizzler
d) Barry Loser
e) Rock Blondsky/Frankie Teacup

Mostly as: You're Barry
Lucky you! You are basikeely the keelest person ever.

Mostly bs: You're Bunky
Good doggy! If you can't be as keel as me then you may as well be
my sidekick. You are loyal and obedient (most of the time).

Mostly cs: You're Nancy
You are often pushing your glasses up your nose and reading.
And you have a black belt in karate.

Mostly ds: You're Sharonella
I'm so sorry.

Mostly es: You're my mum or dad
Or someone else really old.

ADVERTISEMENT

They'rrre disgusting!

Mr Feeko's
Beard Flakes

Please buy some!

Dear Sharonella

Putting the 'agony' in agony aunt.

Yo Shazzles,

How amazingtons are you? Anyway, back to me. I'm worried people at school are getting jelzies of my life.

No names obviously, let's just say Tracy Pilchard and Donnatella have started acting all weird since I got famous.

Without giving anything away, I have a very popular problem page in a newspaper called The Daily Poo and my name's Sharonella.

If there's anyone who can help me I know it's me, I mean you,

Anonymous

xxxxx

Hi Anonymouse, are you a mouse? Ha ha, that's just my sense of humour coming across.

My advice to me, I mean you, is to ignore those two idiots. They're obviously totallyingtons jealous.

Also, if yure reading this, can I have my biro back please Donnatella, unless yuve chewed it up completely.

And by the ways, Trace, your bum looks big in EVRYFING.

Da Shazzles

ADFART
Fronkle Jelly!
with teeth bits!
I ATE TOO MUCH AND NOW I HAVE NO TEETH! (WELL, TWO)
available at
Feeko's
unless sold out

Even more Sketches

Writing a book is a <u>HASSLE</u>.
You have to <u>really think</u> about it.
Just look at Jim's sketchbook pages-
this is his brain trying to make
sense out of all the stupid stuff
floating round inside it...

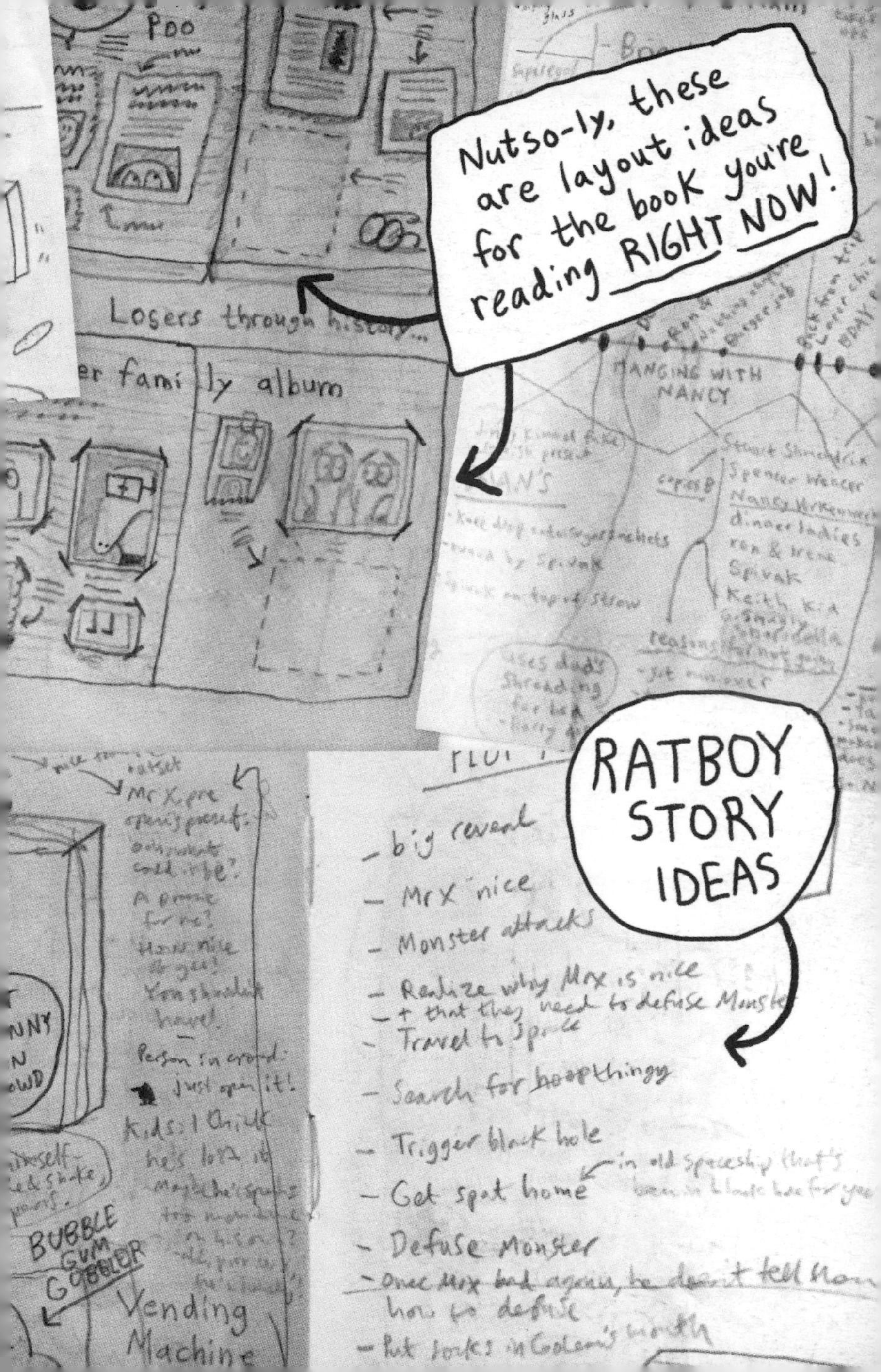

POO

Nutso-ly, these are layout ideas for the book you're reading RIGHT NOW!

Losers through history...

...er family album

HANGING WITH NANCY

Stuart Shmendrik
Spencer Wencer
Nancy Yorkenwork
dinner ladies
ren & irene
Spivak
Keith KIA

reasons for not...

RATBOY STORY IDEAS

- big reveal
- Mr X nice
- Monster attacks
- Realize why Mr X is nice
- + that they need to defuse Monster
- Travel to Space
- Search for hoop thingy
- Trigger black hole
- Get spot home   in old spaceship that's been in black hole for years
- Defuse Monster
- Once Mr X bad again, he doesn't tell how to defuse
- Put socks in Golem's mouth

BUBBLE GUM GOBBLER

Vending Machine

Nigel Zuckerberg's

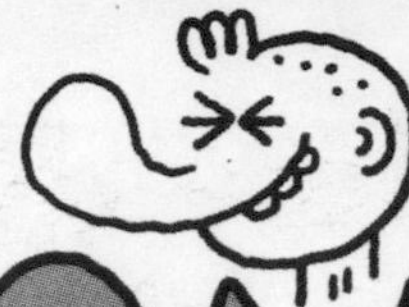

RANDOM JOKES

Did you hear about the massive cheese explosion?
-All that was left was debrie!

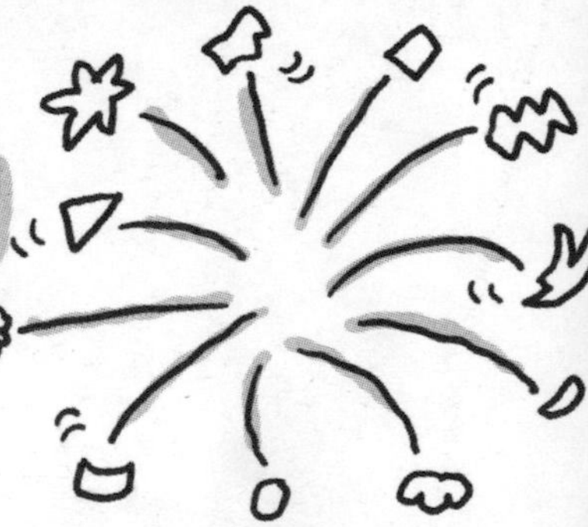

Why is my clock woolly and always spitting at me?

It's an allama clock! →

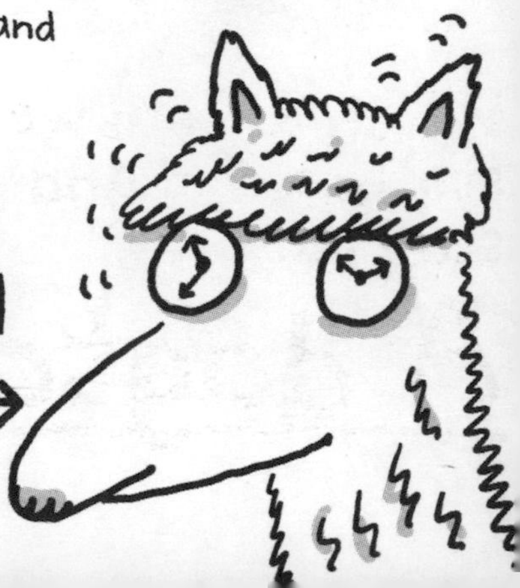

How did the teddy screw in a lightbulb?

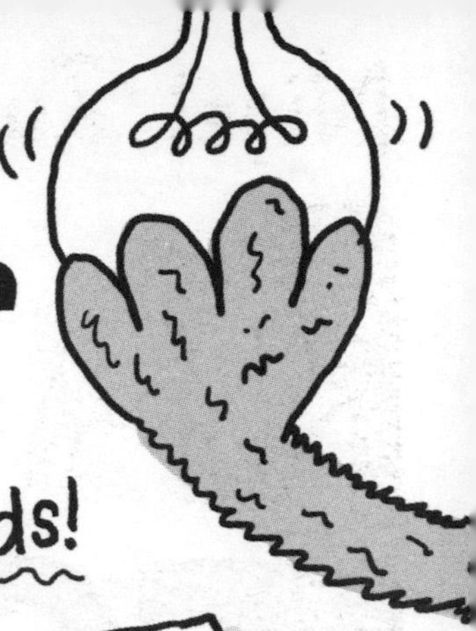

With her bear hands!

UNKY IS THE FUNNIEST.

WHICH FRUIT IS GREAT AT WRITING PLAYS?

William ShakesPEAR

Which animal wears a stethoscope and won't stop barking?

A dogtor!

What are all the animals in the jungle up to?

Just lion around!

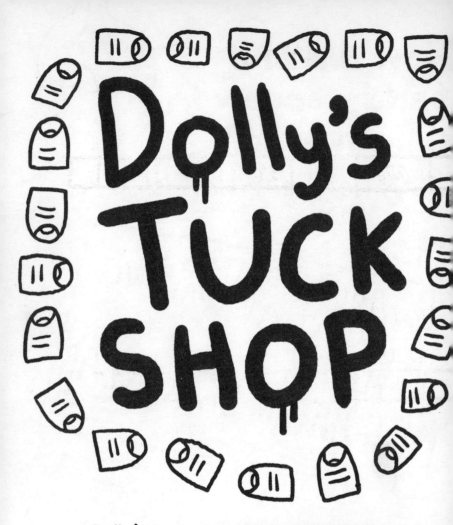

Dolly's TUCK SHOP

Dolly's tuck shop is where all the kids at school get their sweets. But Dolly isn't very imaginative and she only has one type of sweet. Fill the shelves with your own sweet ideas, and make sure they're as keel as Thumb Sweets!

| 27p | | £1.99 | | 12p | |

| 50p | | £2.34 | | 1p | |

| FREE! | | 17p | | £9.99 | |

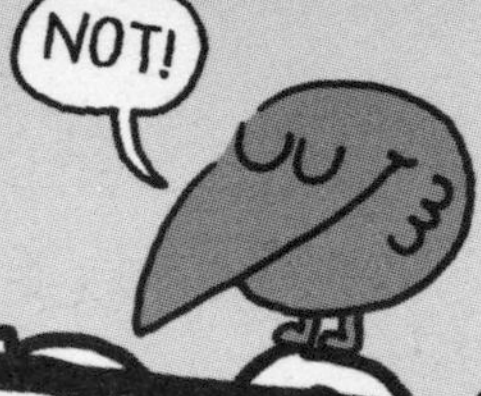
NOT!

~~Knock~~ Knock jokes!

Here are Not Bird's favourite NOT Knock jokes! They're really rubbish!

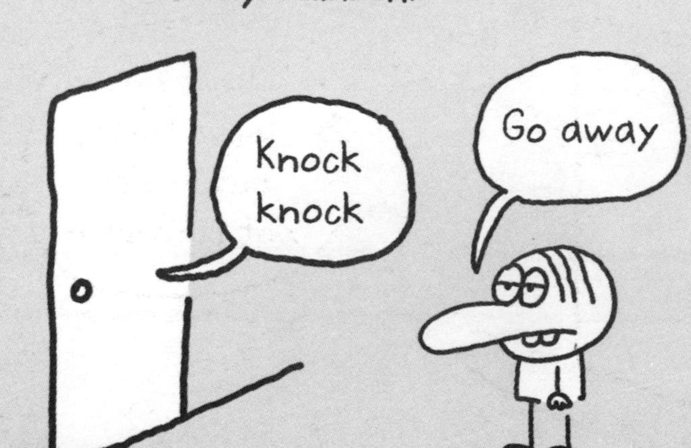
Knock knock
Go away

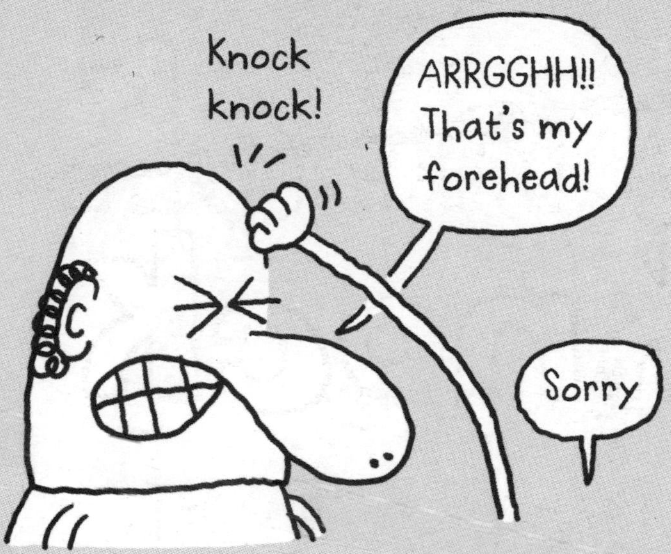
Knock knock!
ARRGGHH!! That's my forehead!
Sorry

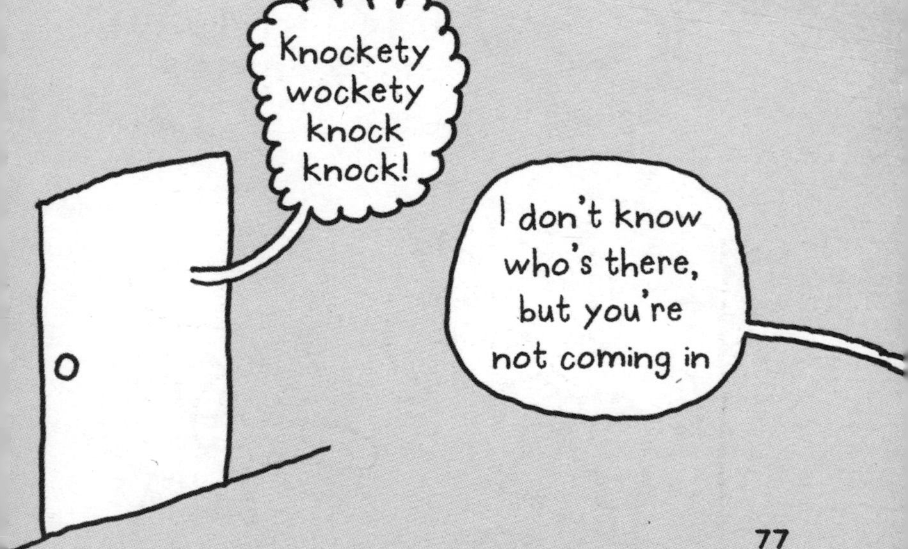
Knockety wockety knock knock!
I don't know who's there, but you're not coming in

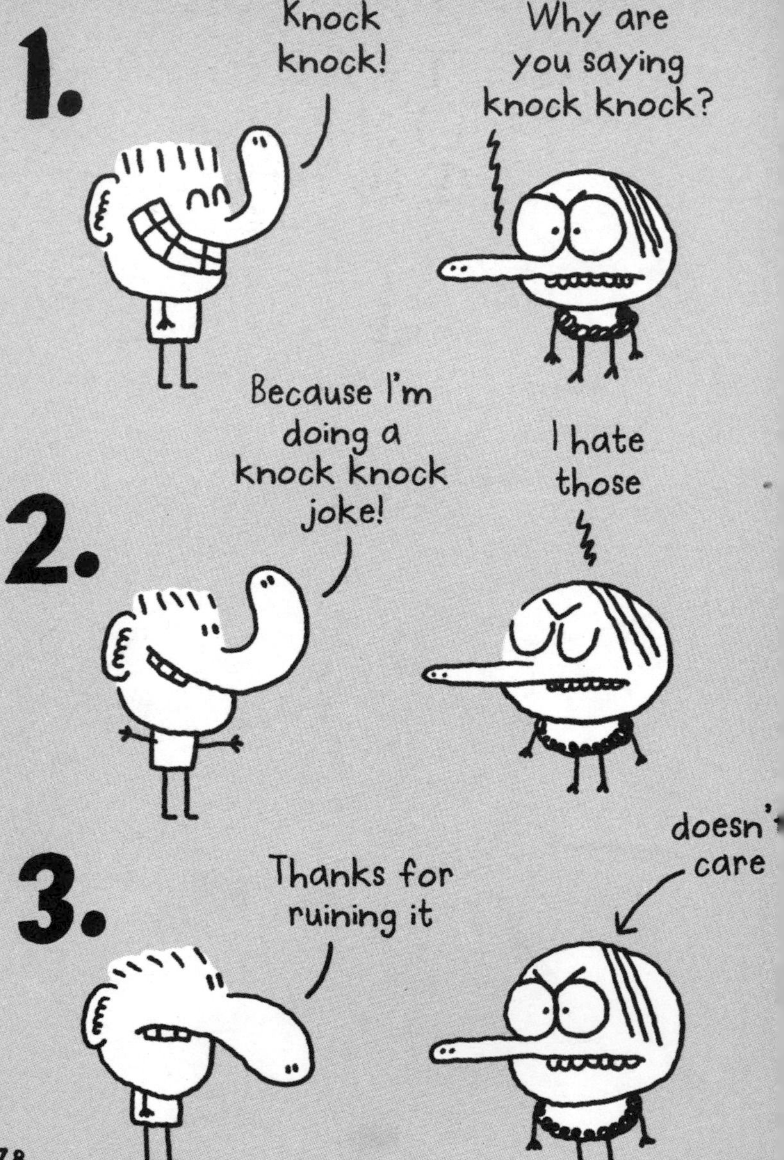
1.
Knock knock!
Why are you saying knock knock?
2.
Because I'm doing a knock knock joke!
I hate those
3.
Thanks for ruining it
doesn't care

WRITE YOUR OWN
REALLY RUBBISH
NOT KNOCK
JOKE HERE!

↓

Ring pulls!

I like ring pulls. I just think they're keel. So I always try and sneak drawings of them into my books. Here are some, turned into other things. Because I'm keel.

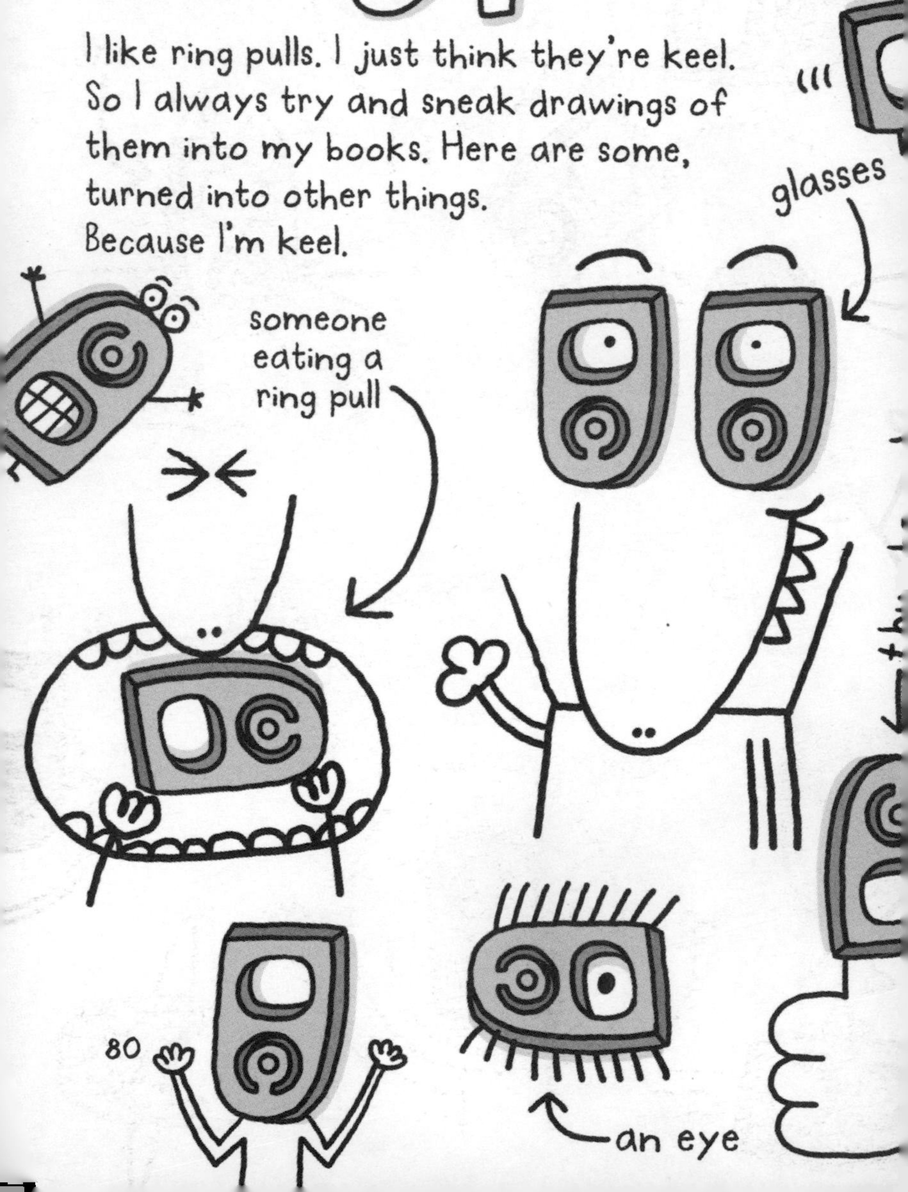
glasses
someone eating a ring pull
an eye

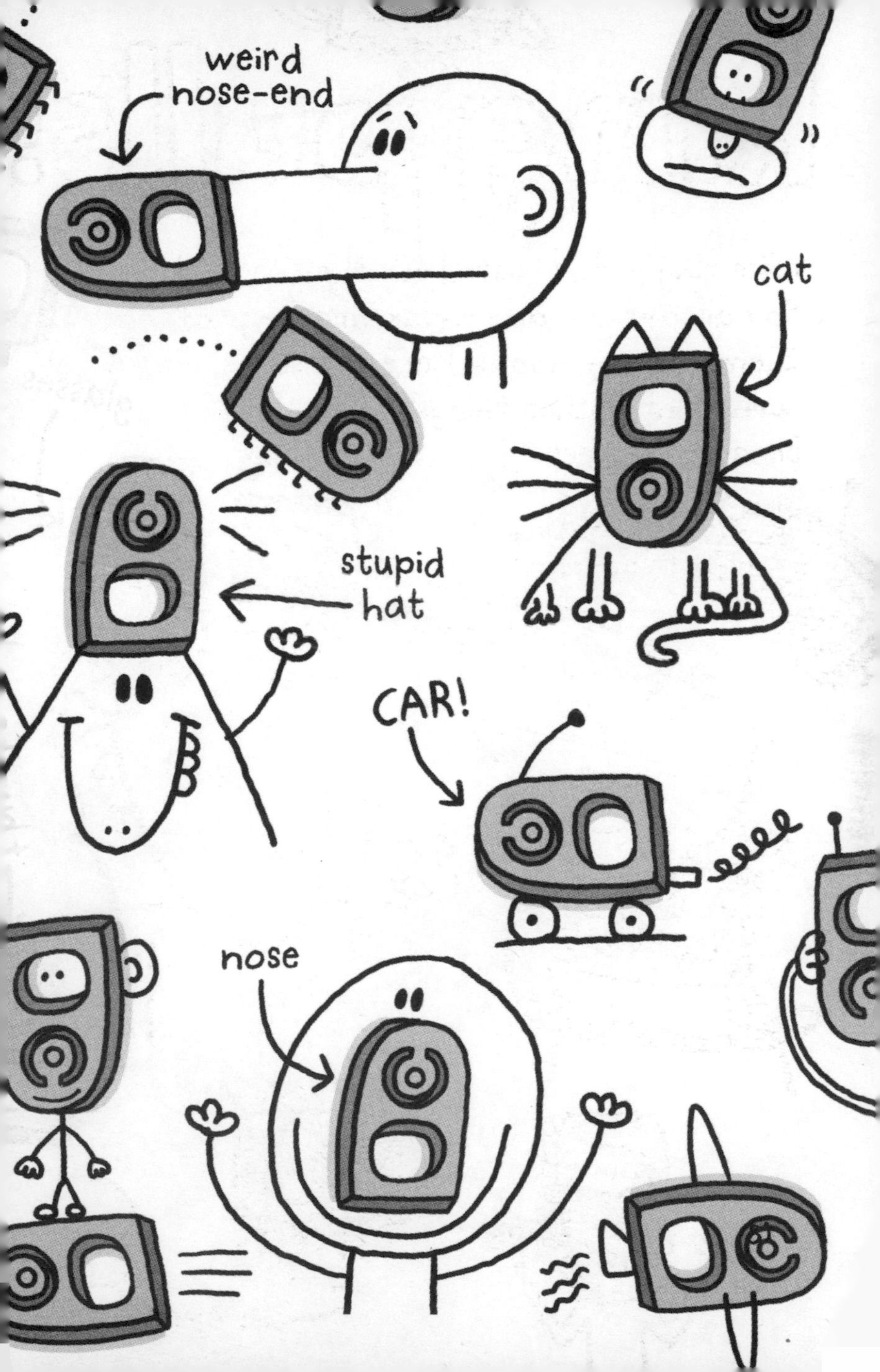
weird nose-end
cat
stupid hat
CAR!
nose

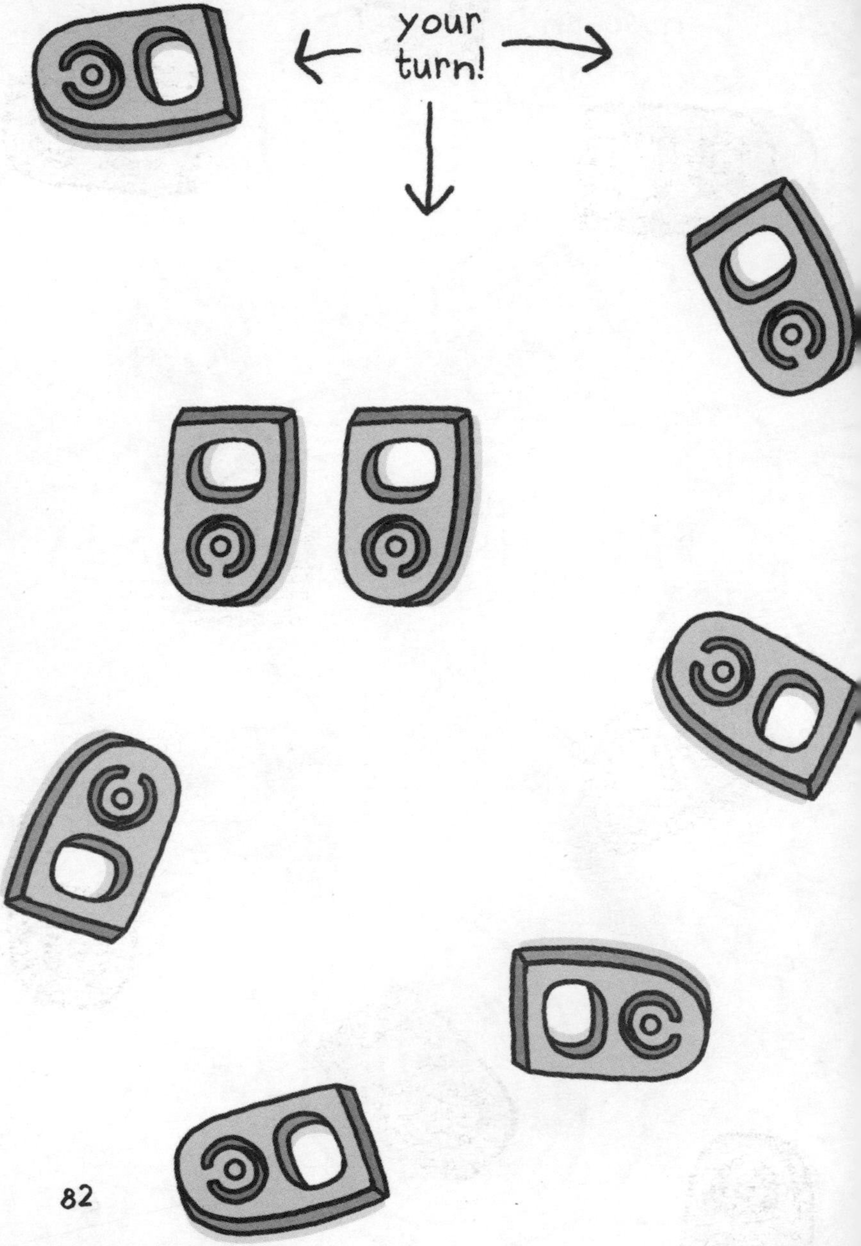
your turn!

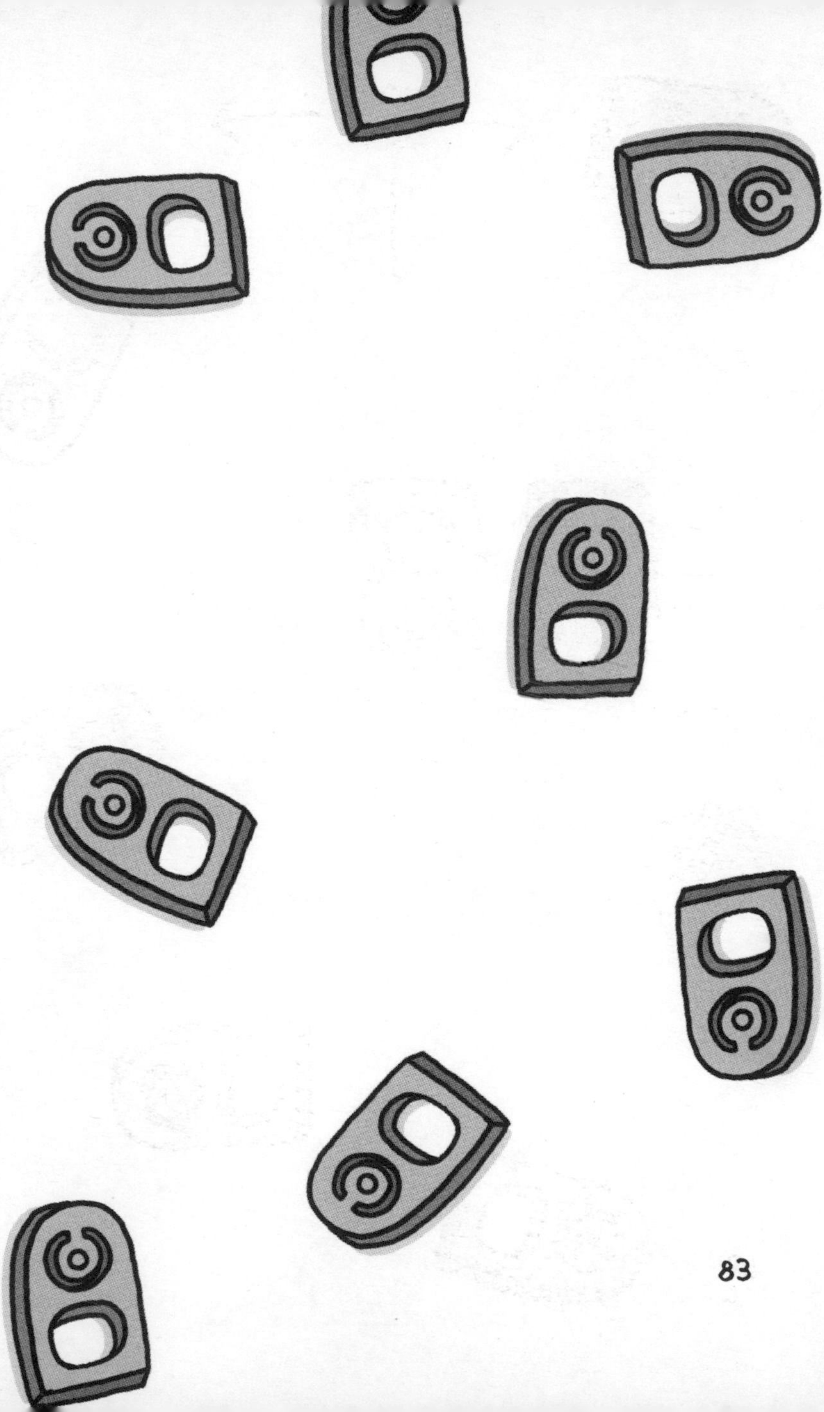

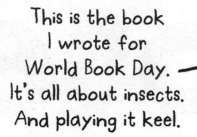

This is the book
I wrote for
World Book Day. ——→
It's all about insects.
And playing it keel.

nit ~~not~~

I am ↑ a Loser

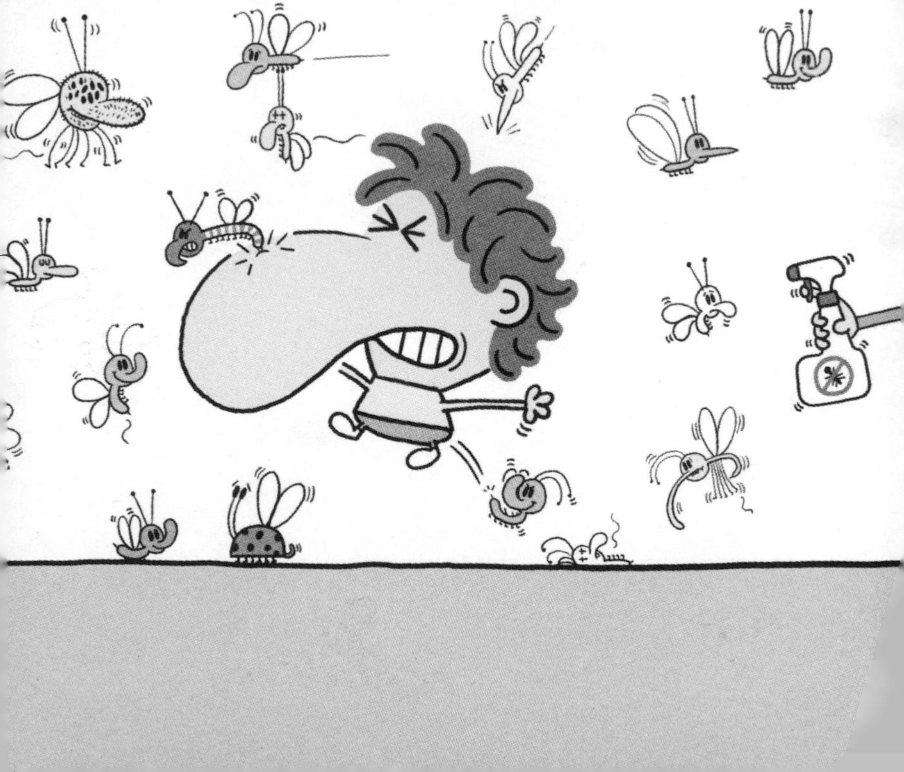

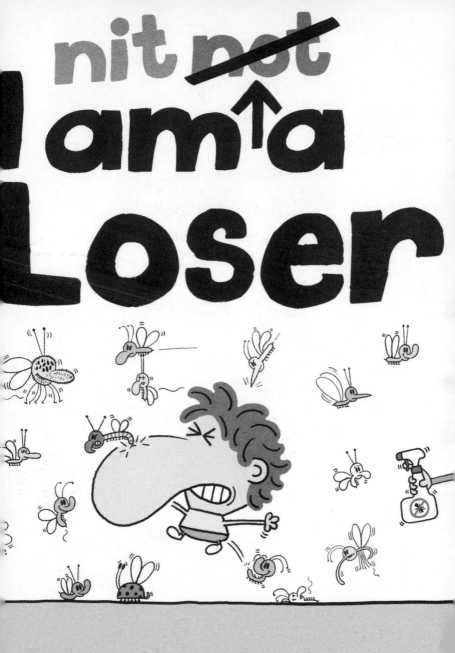

Amazekeel news

Probably the most exciting millisecond in the history of my whole entire life on earth amen was the other day after school when my mum called me into the kitchen.

don't know the news yet

BAARRRYYYY!!!

'Look at this!' she said, holding up the Mogden Gazette. 'Feeko's Supermarkets are bringing out a new shampoo and they're looking for three kids to be in the advert! You could audition with Bunky and Nancy!'

BE A STAR!

excited nose

I jumped in the air and did a dance, and my trousers fell down. Then I picked up the phone and dialled my best friend Bunky's number, which I'm jealous of because it's better than mine.

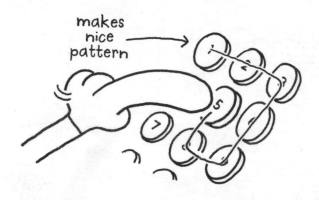

makes nice pattern →

'Bunky! Have you heard?' I screamed when he answered.

'What, have I heard your VOICE?' said Bunky, cracking up at his own stupid joke, but I just ignored him and carried on with what I was saying.

'No you complete loseroid, they're auditioning for a shampoo advert at Feeko's tomorrow!' I snortled, almost weeing myself with excitement.

Bunky

me

I was jiggling around the kitchen like my mum when she dances to the radio, probably because I actually did need a real-life wee really badly.

'Keel!' said Bunky, which is what me and Bunky say instead of 'cool', mostly because it's keeler, but also because it's what they say in our favourite TV show, **Future Ratboy**.

Future Ratboy

his sidekick, Not Bird

I hung up on Bunky and dialled Nancy Verkenwerken's number, which I'm also jealous of, but not as much as Bunky's.

'Nancy! Have you heard?' I said when she answered, except it wasn't Nancy, it was her dad.

'Nancy's round at Bunky's,' said Mr Verkenwerken, so I hung up and phoned Bunky again, jealous of his number AND because Nancy was there.

the wee wiggle

loserish phone cord

'WHAT'S NANCY DOING ROUND YOUR HOUSE WITHOUT ME?' I shouted when Bunky answered the phone, except it wasn't Bunky, it was Nancy.

'I popped in. I do live next door to him, you know,' said Nancy, but I just ignored her and carried on with what I was saying.

Nancy
(obviously)

'Yeah, well, did he tell you the amazekeel news?' I said, stretching the phone cord so I could go for a wee in the toilet, which was across the hall from where I was standing in the kitchen.

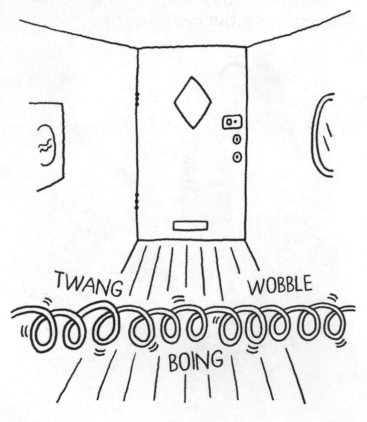

'Yeah, it's keel!' said Nancy, completely copying what me and Bunky say.

Suddenly and boringly my mum walked down the hall, carrying a pile of dirty washing. 'Arrrggghhh!' she screamed, tripping over the phone cord.

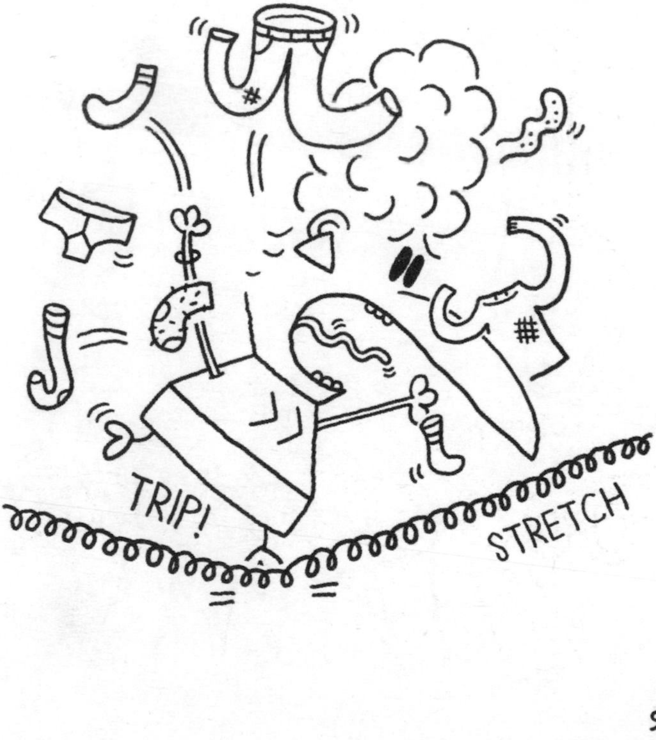
TRIP!
STRETCH

The phone flew out of my hand and I twizzled round like a ballerina. 'See you at Feeko's tomorrow morning. Eight o'clock sharp!' I shouted, wee going everywhere, not that I cared because I was going to be in a shampoo advert!

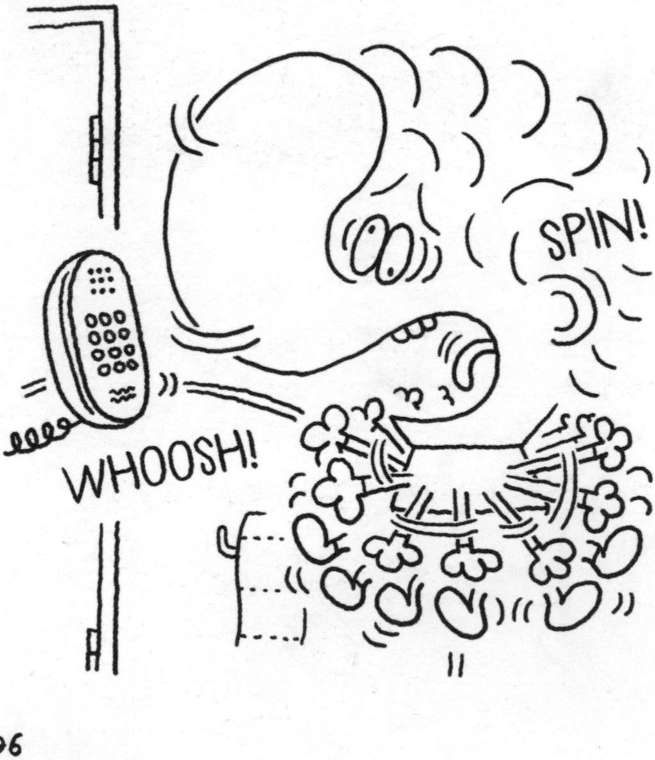
SPIN!
WHOOSH!

Best mood ever

The next morning I sprang out of bed like there was a spring springing me out of it. I looked at the mattress and saw a massive spring springing out of the sheet and realised that a real-life spring had actually sprung me out.

like the phone cord

I chuckled to myself, jumping into the shower with a spring in my step, thinking how it was the first day of spring, which is my favourite season ever, even though I hate the word 'spring' and try not to say it all that much if possible.

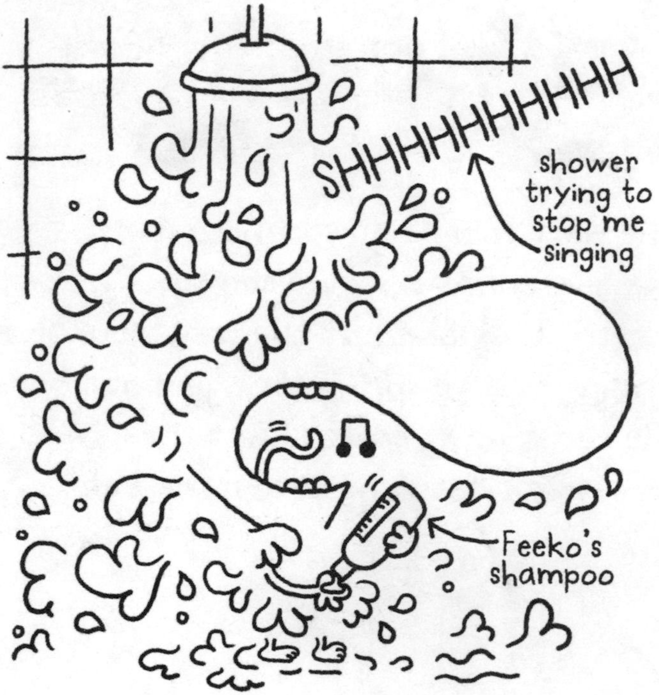
SHHHHHHHHHHHHH
shower trying to stop me singing
Feeko's shampoo

'What's going on here?' said my mum when I came downstairs with my hair all washed and shiny. I think she was a bit surprised, seeing as I usually only have about one shower every eight million years.

'I have to look my best for the shampoo advert!' I said, and my mum did her smile she does when she thinks I'm the best son ever, which I am.

best
son
ever

'Ooh my snuggly little Snookyflumps!' she warbled, giving me a cuddle, which I wriggled out of, even though I secretly quite liked it.

Then I skateboarded off to Feeko's Supermarket, going extra fast because of all the excitement-turbo-blowoffs I was doing.

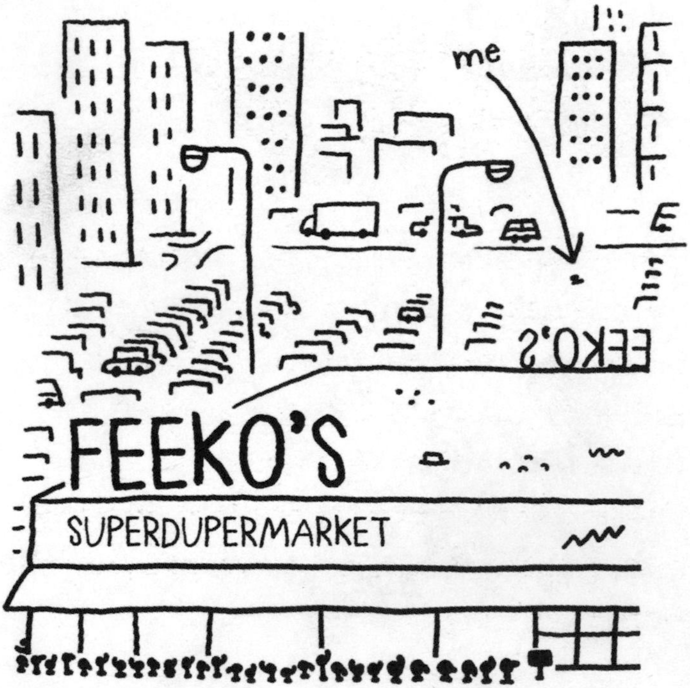
me
FEEKO'S
FEEKO'S
SUPERDUPERMARKET

What a lovely day

'Barry!' shouted Bunky as I skateboarded up to Feeko's playing it keel times a billion and three-quarters. He was halfway down the queue of kids, which was caterpillaring round the building like one of those long wriggly insect things I can never remember the name of.

'You made it!' I smiled, my hair glistening in the sunshine. Nancy strolled up and picked a flower that was growing out of a crack in the pavement, and I gave her a triple-reverse-upside-down-salute, which is what I do when I'm in the best mood ever.

sort of like the mattress spring

'Lovely day, isn't it!' she beamed, sniffing on the flower and sneezing into my face. The sun was beaming in the sky even more than Nancy, and Bunky pulled out a pair of **Future Ratboy** sunglasses.

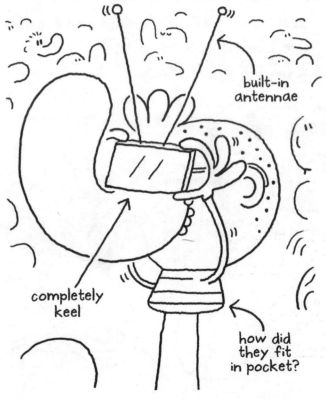

built-in antennae

completely keel

how did they fit in pocket?

'Oh. My. Days. I am LUVVING your shades, Bunky!' said an annoying voice from behind me that sounded just like Sharonella's from our class at school.

I turned round and did a blowoff out of shock, because it actually WAS Sharonella, not that I should have been all that surprised, seeing as the voice had sounded EX-ACK-ER-LY like hers.

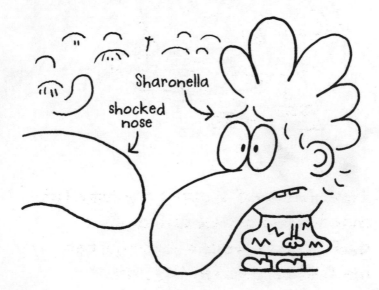

Sharonella

shocked nose

'Helloooo, Darren fans!' said Darren
Darrenofski, who I hadn't spotted
because he was standing behind
Sharonella, and I did another blowoff
because of how annoying he is too.

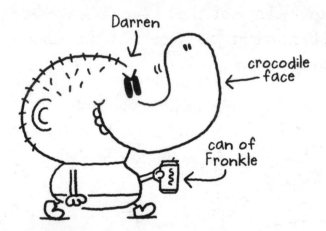

Darren

crocodile
face

can of
Fronkle

'Next five kids!' shouted a spotty fat
man holding a clipboard, and we
shuffled into Feeko's Supermarket,
me first because I'm the best.

The store room

'This way,' shouted the clipboard man, walking us through Feeko's, which was full of grannies and grandads doing their boring old Saturday morning shopping.

Right at the back of the store was an enormous metal door with a yellow poster on it saying 'Nit Shampoo Auditions Here!'

'Nit shampoo? You didn't say it was for NIT SHAMPOO!' said Bunky, pointing at the poster, then poking me in the nose with the finger he'd just been pointing at the poster with.

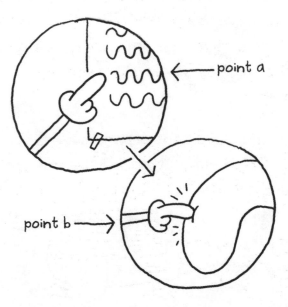

point a

point b

'Oh well, we're here now!' I smiled, thinking how I should be in a good mood more often, and I pushed the door open and walked through.

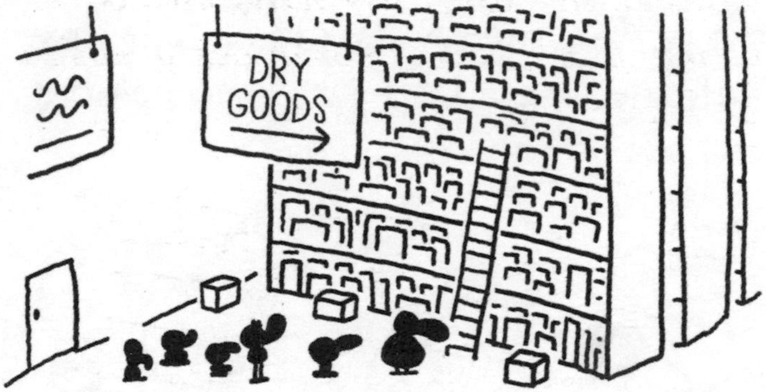
DRY
GOODS

We were in the storeroom, which was like a whole nother Feeko's, except much colder and without any customers. It had all the same stuff stacked up in cardboard boxes, on shelves eight million times the height of normal ones.

The clipboard man walked us over to the shampoo aisle and told us to wait there, then walked off again, his footsteps echoing.

It was boring just standing there waiting, so I stuck my hand into a cardboard box and pulled out a bottle of Feeko's Cherry Shampoo.

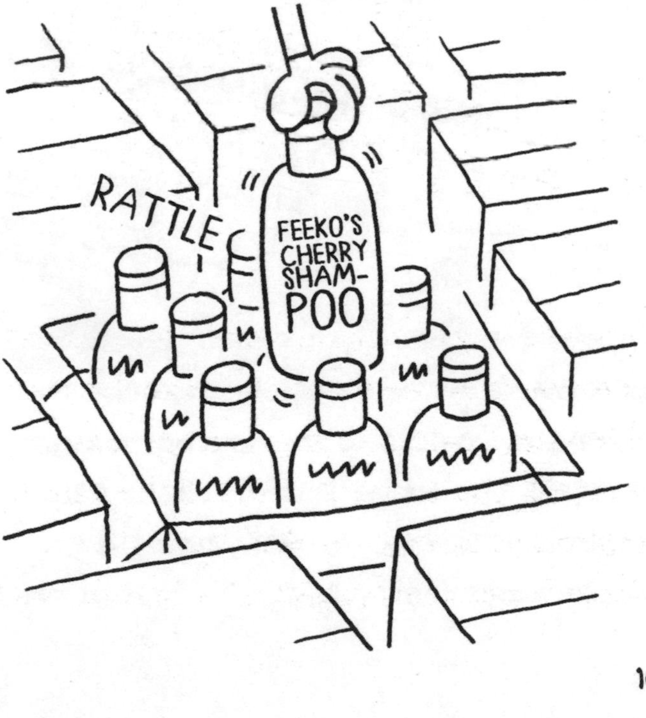
RATTLE
FEEKO'S CHERRY SHAM-POO

I covered the 'SHAM' bit with my finger and put on my advert face. 'Mmm, Feeko's Cherry poo!' I snortled, and Bunky and Nancy weed themselves with laughter.

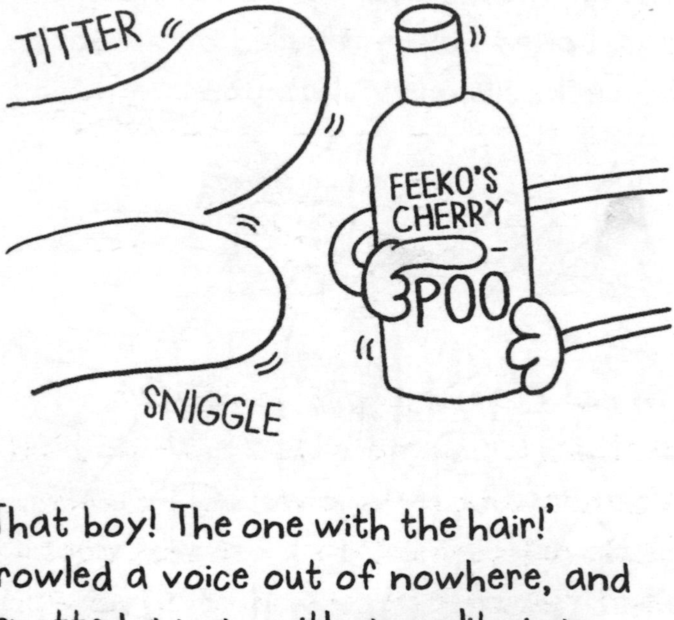
TITTER
FEEKO'S
CHERRY
POO
SNIGGLE

'That boy! The one with the hair!' growled a voice out of nowhere, and I spotted a man with an unlit cigar hanging out of his mouth, pointing at me. 'He's perfect!'

that man I was just talking about

I'm not used to people saying I'm perfect, so I jumped in the air and did a dance, and my trousers fell down. 'Little old keelness me?' I smiled, copying what **Future Ratboy** said when he won 'Keelest Person Ever' at the TV Awards last year.

The clipboard man walked over and bent down. 'The director would like to see you first,' he whispered in my ear, his voice going right through my brain and out the other ear, into one of Nancy's.

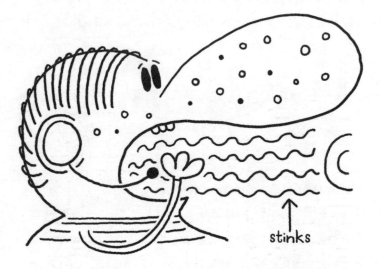

stinks

'What about me and Bunky?' Nancy said, looking all sad.

I looked over at my best friends and felt sorry for them for not being as brilliant as me.

'I don't go anywhere without these two!' I said, and we walked over to the director together, me first again, because I'm the keelest, like I said earlier.

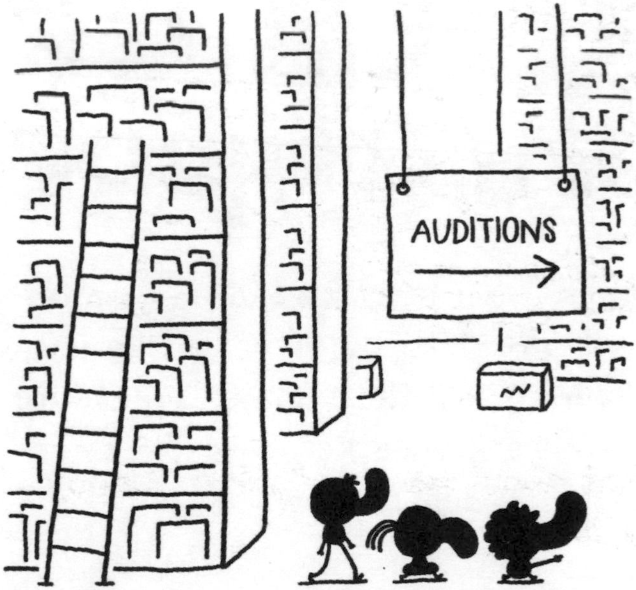
AUDITIONS

Feeko's Nit Shampoo

'Names?' said a frizzy-haired woman standing next to the director. Nancy and Bunky said their names, which are 'Nancy Verkenwerken' and 'Bunky' in case you didn't know.

'Barry Loser,' I said, smiling like I was in an advert for being Barry Loser.

'Barry Loser? That's hilarious!' chuckled the director, and everyone laughed, including Darren and Sharonella, who were standing at the edge waiting for their go.

clipboard man

I snortled, feeling like I was in one of those dreams where everything's going really well, and the frizzy-haired woman nudged us into the middle of the aisle.

'Just walk a bit, as if you're going down the street . . .' she said, looking at my hair all jealously.

116

I glanced at Bunky, who's sort of like my pet dog, then at Nancy, who's sort of like my pet cat, which sort of made me their leader, which meant I'd better say something.

'Bunky, Nancy,' I said, putting my arms round them, 'let's give this a hundred and twenty million billion percent!' I whispered, copying what they say on my mum's favourite TV talent show. I put my hand up and we all high fived, and it echoed round the storeroom.

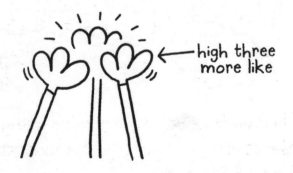

← high three more like

Nancy started to stroll, twiddling her flower and looking up at the ceiling lights as if they were the sun. 'What a lovely day!' she beamed.

'Yes, isn't it glorious!' I said, glancing up at the fake sun and snatching Bunky's **Future Ratboy** sunglasses off his face. 'If only I didn't have these pesky nits in my hair . . .'

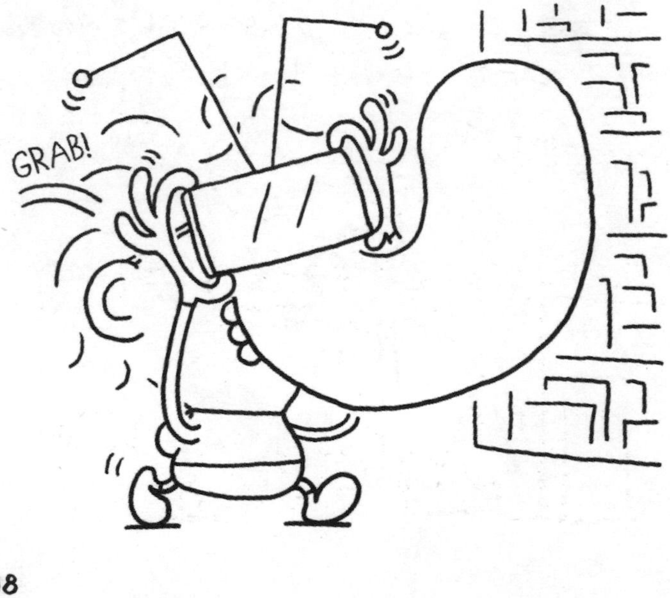
GRAB!

The director chuckled and the frizzy-haired woman jotted something down in her notebook.

'Can't . . . see . . .' mumbled Bunky, squinting from his no sunglasses. He stumbled into a shelf and a cardboard box crashed to the floor, shampoo bottles flying everywhere.

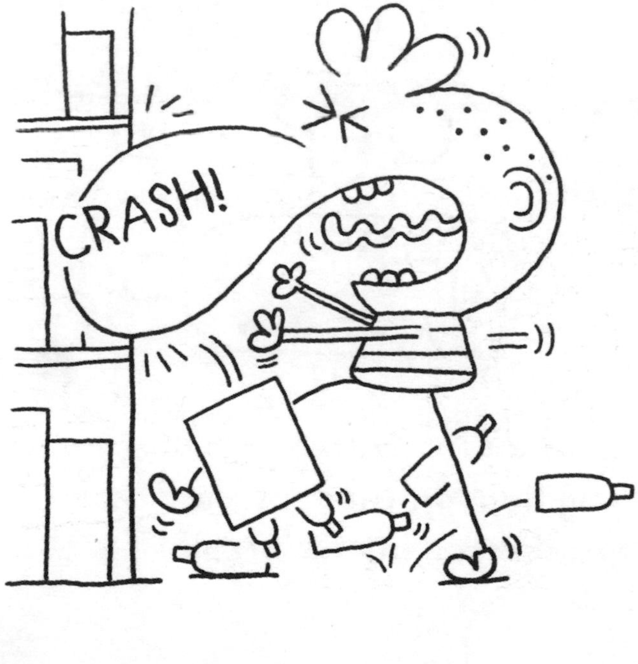
CRASH!

'Hmmm . . .' grumbled the director, and the frizzy-haired woman jotted something else down in her notebook, but not in a good way. I bent over, worried Bunky was ruining everything, and picked up a bottle of almond conditioner.

pretending he's dead so I don't pick him up

'Ooh, Feeko's Nit Shampoo,' I said, totally making it up on the spot. 'Just the thingypoos for my nit problem!'

I flipped the lid open, held it over my head and squeezed. Light-brown slime drizzled on to my hair and down my face.

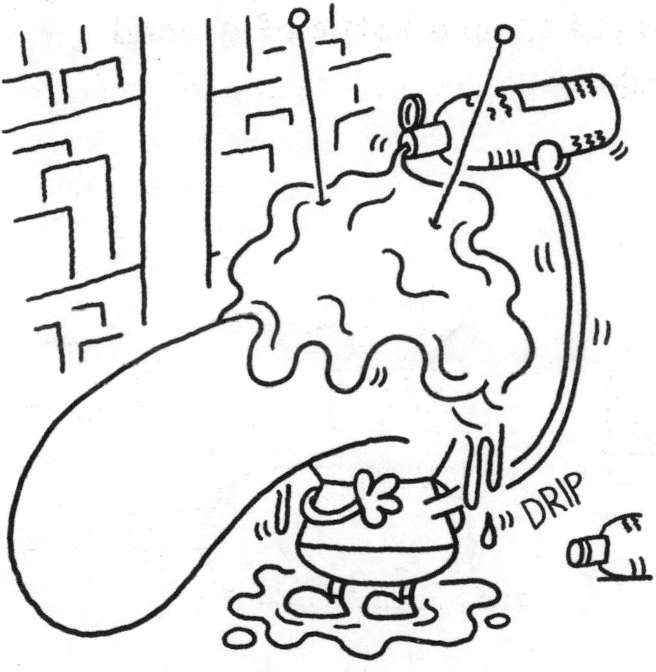
DRIP

'Feeko's Nit Shampoo,' I said, doing my best advert voice. 'Because it's keel!'

There was a millisecond of silence like you get in-between adverts on the telly, then the director stood up.

'Bravo!' he roared, and everyone in the whole shampoo aisle applauded, including me, because I'm my number-one fan.

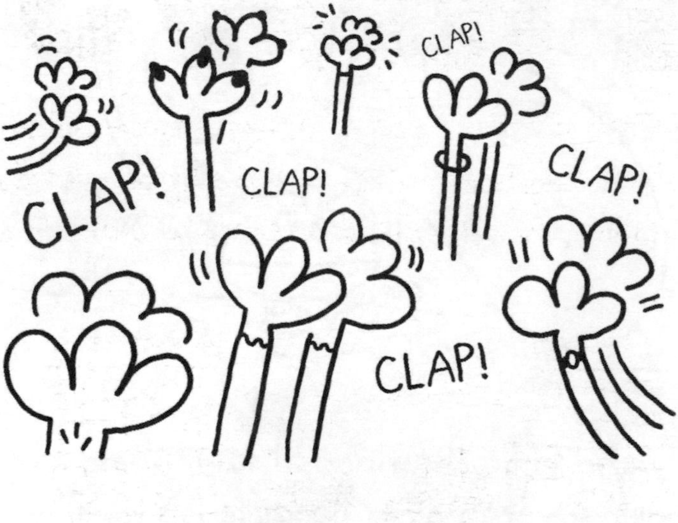
CLAP!
CLAP!
CLAP!
CLAP!
CLAP!

Even more amazekeel news

After that we sat through seven billion other auditions which were all completely rubbish, including Sharonella and Darren's.

Yay, shampoo!

Yeah, yay

Then the director whispered something into the frizzy-haired woman's ear and she clapped her hands, but not like she was clapping someone, more to shut us up.

normal clap

shush clap

'Thank you all for coming today. It's been SO hard to decide!' she shouted, which is what they always say at things like this, just to make the losers feel better. 'However, the three winners have been chosen, and they are . . . Barry Loser, Nancy Verkenwerken and Bunky!'

You know how I said the most exciting millisecond in the history of my whole entire life on earth amen was when my mum told me about the shampoo auditions? That was until right now.

'YIPPEE-KEEL-KAYAY!' I screamed, jumping in the air with Nancy and Bunky, and we all did a dance, and my trousers fell down.

shampoo
wiped off

A week later

It was a week later and my mum was dropping me, Bunky and Nancy off to film the advert.

'See you later for your big camping trip!' said my mum, because we were sleeping in the tent in my back garden that night to celebrate being famous.

TRUNDLE

'OK, Mrs Bunky!' I shouted, pretending she was Bunky's mum because of how embarrassing she is, and she ruffled my hair.

The advert was being filmed down the poshest street in Mogden, which was sort of like the shampoo aisle in Feeko's storeroom except the cardboard boxes were enormous houses, and instead of fake sun there was cloud.

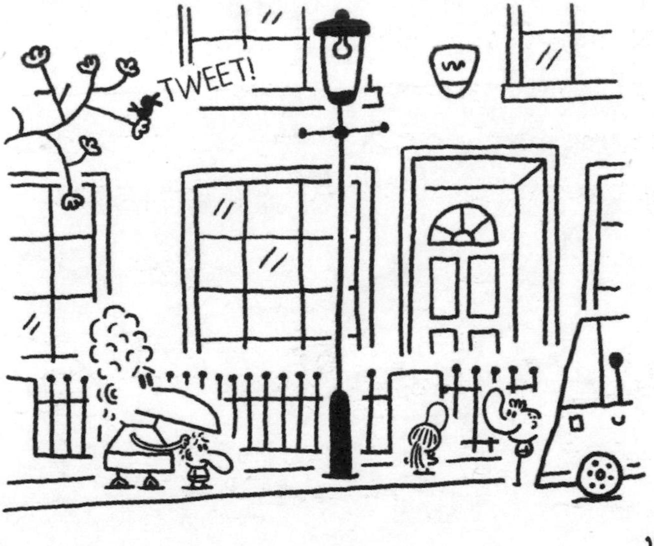
TWEET!

Darren Darrenofski wobbled up, sipping on a can of Fronkle. 'Good mornkeels, Darren fans!' he burped, and I spotted something Sharonella-ish behind him.

'What in the name of unkeelness are YOU TWO doing here?' I said, patting my hair down where my mum had just ruffled it.

'We're spectatoring!' said Sharonella, and I felt sorry for them, not being the stars of a nit shampoo advert like me.

Darren's nose

Sharonella's whole head

my nose

The director walked over and ruffled
my hair right where I'd just patted it
down.

'Hey kids! I had the greatest idea for
the advert last night,' he said, all
excitedly. 'It's got everything - energy,
passion, FIZZAZZ!'

fizzazz

'What IS it?' said Sharonella, even
though it was none of her business.

'One word: ROLLER SKATES!' he boomed, and I gulped, because I'd never roller skated in my life.

'That's two words,' said Nancy, and I trod on her foot to shut her up.

'One, two, what's the difference?' breathed the director, blowing a cloud of cigar smoke into my face.

mixed with really bad breath

FFFFFFFFF

130

I thought about my skateboard, and how roller skating is probably just like riding two skateboards instead of one.

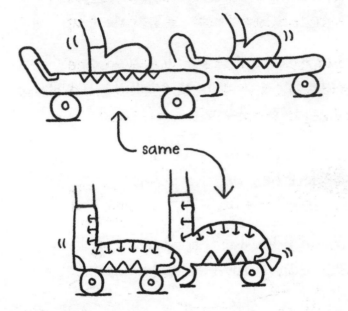

same

'Yeah Nancy, what's the difference?' I said, and she trod on BOTH my feet to shut me up.

Runaway Loser

Frizzy hair gave us all a pair of roller skates and a helmet each. I put mine on and stood up.

You know how I said the advert was being filmed on the poshest street in Mogden? It's also the hilliest.

'Waaaahhhhh!!!' I screamed, rolling backwards down a huge slope.

ZOOM!

'We have a runaway Loser,' said Clipboard man into a walkie-talkie, and everybody laughed.

'Barrrryyyyy!' cried Nancy, zooming after me on her roller skates, with Bunky right behind. They sped past and looped back, stretching their arms out and holding hands to catch me.

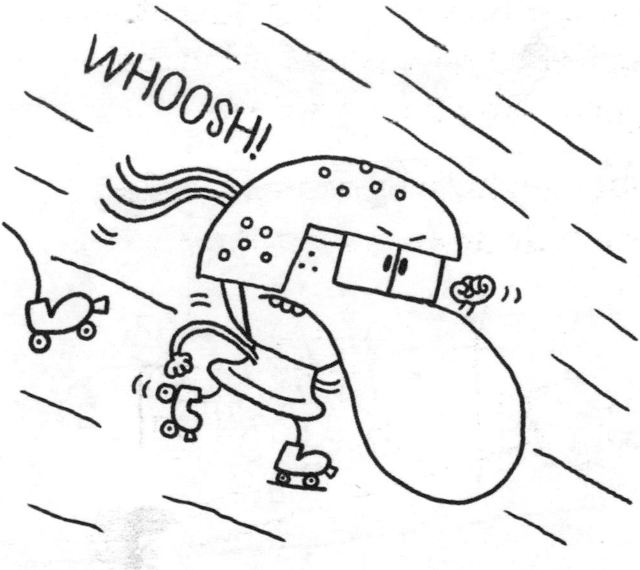
WHOOSH!

'Uunnggfh!' I blurted, crashing into them, and we all fell over.

I stood up, wobblingly, and patted my hair down for the eight millionth time that morning, even though it was inside a helmet. 'Let's film this advert!' I boomed, trying to sound like their leader, and I fell straight down on my bum again.

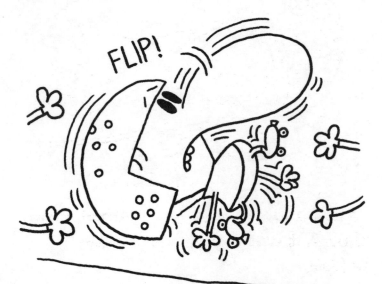

FLIP!

Action

'Aaaaannnnddd . . . ACTION!' boomed
the director, and Nancy started to
roller skate down the road.

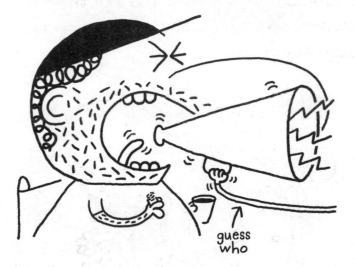

guess
who

'What a lovely day!' she beamed, even
though it was even cloudier than
before.

'Isn't it glorious!' I warbled, wobbling behind her, my arms waggling to keep steady. 'If only I didn't have these pesky nits doing poos all over my head.' I rolled past the camera and crashed into the frizzy-haired woman.

two seconds before crash

'CUT!' growled the director. 'Barry baby, where's the magic gone?' he said, blowing cigar smoke in my face AGAIN.

A huge black cloud had appeared behind him, and I imagined a giant director out in space, blowing cigar smoke on to the world.

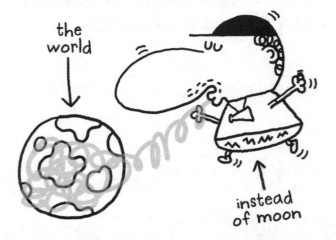

the world

instead of moon

I tried to stand up, but my feet were skidding off in opposite directions. Bunky and Nancy rolled over and dragged me to the kerb. 'You OK Barry?' said Nancy, and I gave her a thumbs up, mostly because I was too out of breath to speak.

'OK, let's go again,' shouted the director. 'Really work it this time, guys. Aaaaannnnddd . . . ACTION!'

'What a LUVVERLY day!' said Nancy, and Bunky twizzled round like a ballerina.

'Isn't it glorious!' I said, zooming past them and tripping over a camera wire. 'ARRGGHHH!!!' I screamed, flying through the air and landing in a bush.

SHLUMPF!

'Maybe we could get rid of the roller skates?' I heard the frizzy-haired woman say to the director, her voice muffled from all the leaves around my ears.

The air had turned cold, like in the storeroom at Feeko's.

'What, and lose the FIZZAZZ?!' growled the director. He looked at his watch, then the big black cloud, and shook his head.

rain o'clock

'Is there anyone else here who can roller skate?' asked the director.

'Me!' shouted Darren Darrenofski before I'd even clambered out of the bush.

LEAP!

Thunder and lightning

'Help me!' I wailed, trying to get up, my feet running away from their owner, who was me.

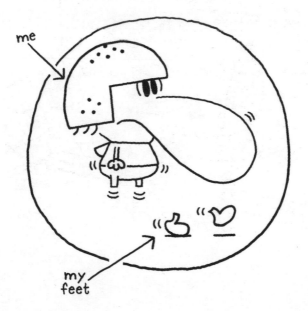

me

my feet

Darren was squidging his fat little feet into a spare pair of roller skates as Bunky and Nancy glided towards me. They grabbed a Barry-arm each and rolled me over to the director.

'You've got to give him one more chance!' said Nancy, holding me up like an old grandad who can't walk.

WOBBLE

Lightning struck in the distance as Darren trundled past doing a little jump. 'Barry baby, what can I tell you,' sighed the director. 'I've gotta get this thing filmed before the rain starts. I'm sorry, really I am.'

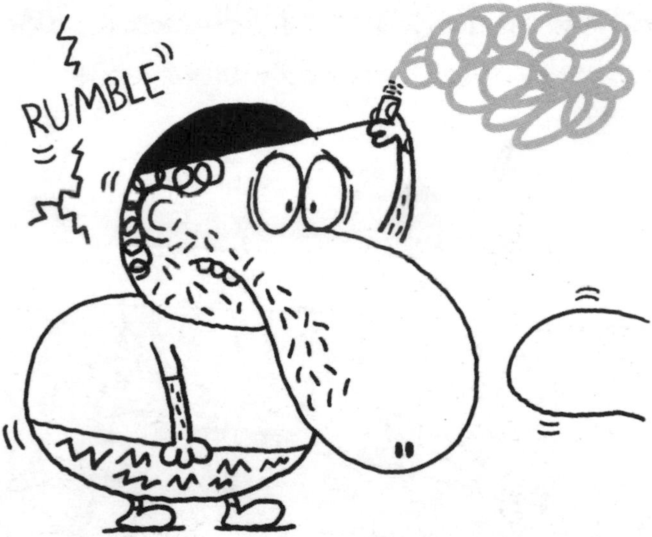
RUMBLE

My knees gave way and I collapsed to the floor like an empty Feeko's carrier bag. 'But you said I was perfect!' I cried.

I lay on the ground, thinking how this whole auditioning thing had been my idea in the first place.

'BUNKY, NANCY, I ORDER YOU NOT TO BE IN THE NIT SHAMPOO ADVERT WITHOUT YOUR LEADER!' I roared, but in a nice way, and waited for them both to say 'OK' and take off their roller skates.

CRACK!

144

Bunky looked at me all guiltily, like a dog just before it's about to do a poo right in the middle of the pavement.

naughty Bunky

Nancy glided over, her ponytail swishing like a cat's tail. She held my hand in hers and looked me in the eyes, then glanced towards the director.

BZZZ—

'I'm so sorry Barry,' she said, turning round and floating away, and I did the angriest blowoff in the history of angry blowoffs ever. Or maybe it was just the thunder.

The long walk home

It was a long walk home in the rain from the posh street to my house, especially with Sharonella bobbling along next to me for half of it, going on about how we were the only two people not in a nit shampoo advert.

'Forget about that lot, Barry. Who needs 'em, that's what I say!' she wheezed, huffing and puffing to keep up, but I just ignored her and carried on with what I was doing.

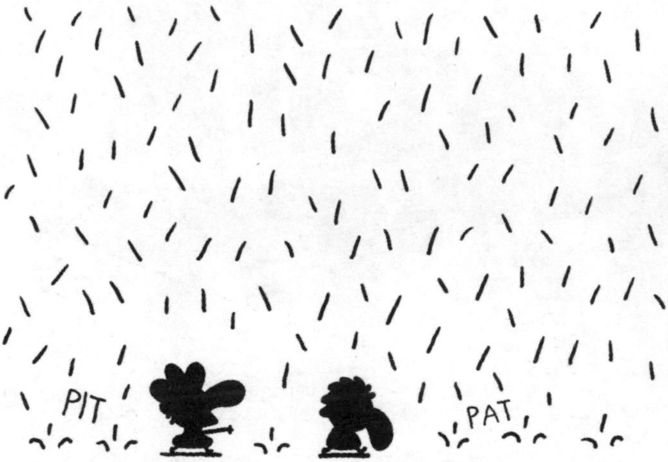
PIT
PAT

I was soaking wet by the time I got to my front door. 'What's happened to my Snookyflumps?' chuckled my mum as the clouds parted and the sun came out behind me.

I barged past her up to my bedroom and started packing my rucksack. 'Barrypoos, are you OK?' she warbled, her knees clicking as she climbed the stairs.

I grabbed my cuddly **Future Ratboy** and stuffed him into the bag, looking out the window at the tent that me, Bunky and Nancy were supposed to be camping in tonight, to celebrate being famous.

'Where are Bunky and Nancy?' said my mum, and I thought of them celebrating with Darren, somewhere else.

I swung the rucksack over my shoulder and stomped downstairs, straight towards the tent.

'SEE YOU IN A MILLION YEARS,' I shouted to everyone in the whole wide world, and I zipped the floppy door shut behind me.

ZZZIP!

Camping on my ownypoos

I lay down on my sleeping bag and closed my eyes, trying to forget about it all, and felt something tickle my face.

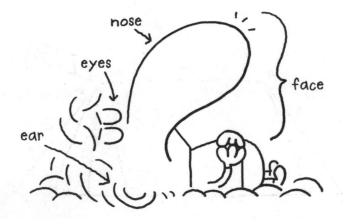

nose

eyes

ear

face

'ARRRGGGHHH! SPIDER!' I screamed,
unzipping the door and rolling on to
the wet grass. I scrabbled at my nose,
which was where the tickle was, and
a sleeping bag feather floated off it,
into the sky.

I tutted to myself, crawling back inside
the tent, and lay down with my head
sticking out like a dog in his kennel. The
whole garden was glistening now, sun
reflecting off the wet leaves and into
my eyes.

One of those insect things with seven trillion legs trundled past, smiling. 'What are YOU so happy about?' I mumbled.

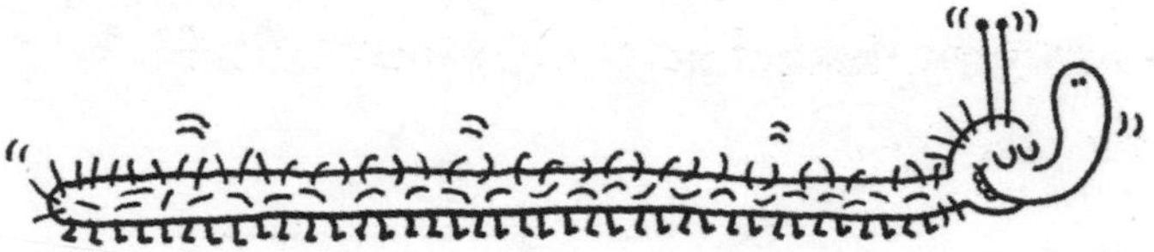

Three centimetres away an ant was busy dragging his dead ant-friend down a tiny little hole in the earth.

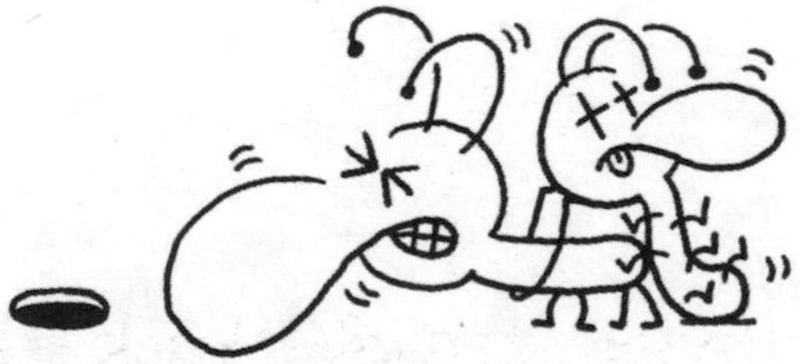

'You wouldn't abandon YOUR leader, would you, Mr Ant?' I whispered to him in my best insect voice.

I looked around at all the millions of other insects pottering about, minding their own businesses, and thought how sweet they were, eating leaves and doing the tiniest poos ever.

And then it hit me.

What had I been thinking, wanting to be in a Feeko's Nit Shampoo advert? I wasn't an insect murderer!

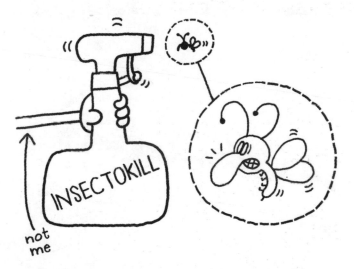

Who did Nancy and Bunky reckon they were, roller skating around with Darren Darrenofski, telling people to kill innocent little bugs!

'Snackypoos, Snookyflumps!' chirped my mum, knocking on the tent and passing me a plate of chocolate digestives. 'Bunky and Nancy phoned ... I said you'd call them when you were ready.'

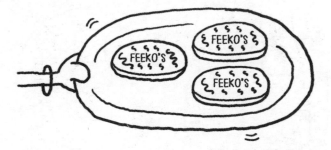

I looked at the Feeko's logo stamped into the biscuits, and thought of my evil insect-killing ex-best-friends with their keeler-than-mine phone numbers, starring in their stupid nit shampoo advert.

'Fanks, Mumsy,' I said, taking a bite of one, and twelve billion crumbs scattered on to the grass. 'Who needs 'em!' I whispered in my insect voice, settling down to dinner with my millions of tiny new best friends.

Insect
murderers

All of a non-sudden it was Monday and I was skateboarding to school through Mogden Common, which is this massive bit of grass in the middle of town where everyone takes their dogs to do poos.

TREMBLE

A butterfly was flitter-fluttering next to my head like a miniature fan, his tiny wings cooling me off in the morning sun, when I spotted a worm wriggling across the pavement.

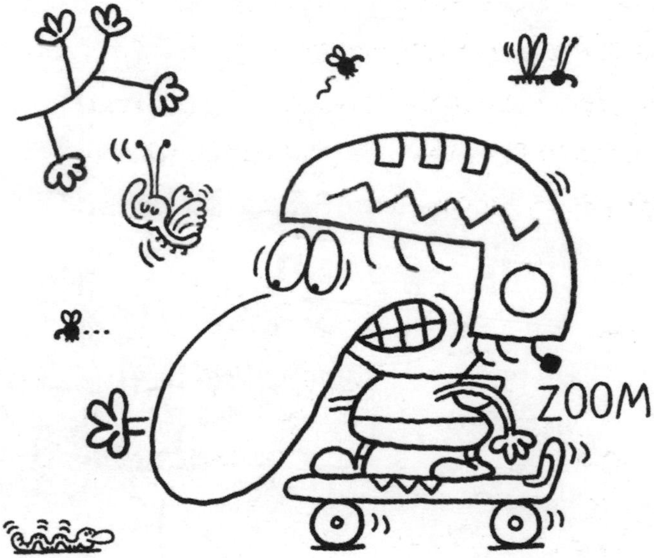
ZOOM

'EEEKK!' I shrieked, swerving to miss him and crashing nose-first into a billboard.

'FEEKO'S NIT SHAMPOO KILLS NITS DEAD!' said the headline on the poster. Underneath there was a photo of Bunky, Nancy and Darren roller skating down the road, looking all happy and nit-free.

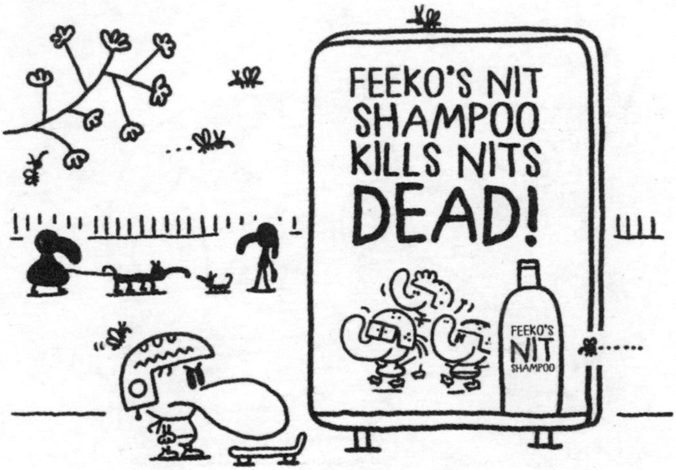
FEEKO'S NIT SHAMPOO KILLS NITS DEAD!
FEEKO'S NIT SHAMPOO

'Insect murderers!' I grumbled, standing up, and a fly flew right into my eyeball, completely and utterly blinding me.

'Good!' I mumbled, because I didn't have to look at that stupid advert any more. Then I realised it wasn't good, because I'd accidentally killed a fly.

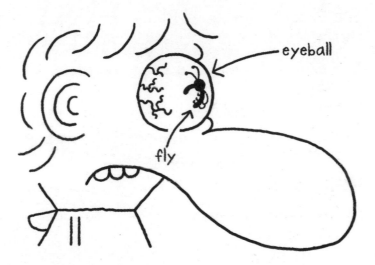

I rubbed my eye and looked into my hand. The fly was curled up, drowned in my tears, his little wings stuck to his body like my clothes after that walk home in the rain the other day.

'I'm sorry, Mr Fly,' I said, kneeling down and scraping a hole in the dirt. I plopped him in and put the dirt back, then picked up an old lolly stick that was lying on the pavement and broke the end off to make a gravestone.

I grabbed a pencil out of my rucksack and wrote 'FLY' in tiny capitals on the bit of wood. 'May you rest in keelness,' I said, digging the mini gravestone into the dirt and heading off for school.

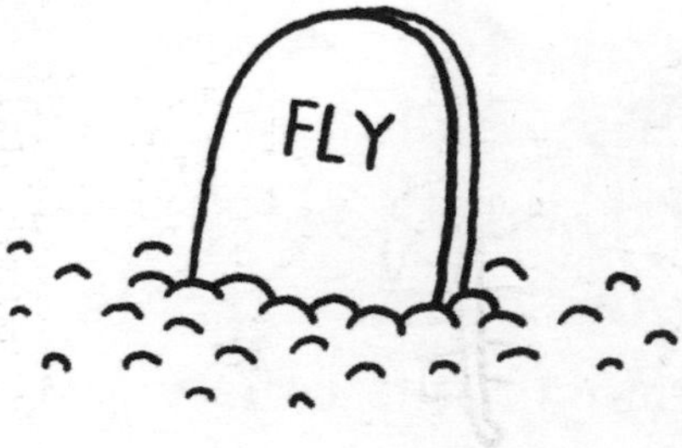
FLY

Nits are the keelest

The annoying thing about being the nicest, most non-insect-killing person in the whole wide world amen is that you have to stop every two minutes to bury all the insects you keep accidentally killing.

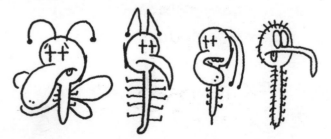

Like the ant I ran over with my skateboard three seconds after I'd drowned that fly in my eyeball. And the daddy-long-legs I swallowed while yawning eight milliseconds after that.

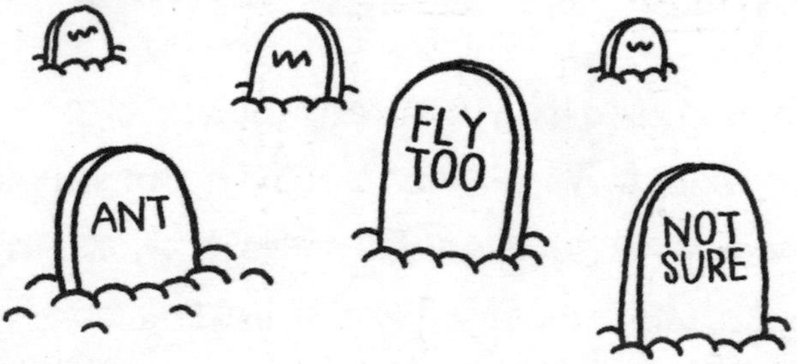
FLY TOO
ANT
NOT SURE

By the time I got to school I'd had to do so many insect funerals that I'd used up four lolly sticks and my pencil lead was completely worn down.

There was a crowd around Bunky
and Nancy as I walked through the
classroom door, everyone asking them
about the advert and whether they
were millionaires yet.

walking
through
door
(get it?)

'Barry!' said Bunky, walking over to me
all guiltily like a dog that's just done a
wee in the middle of the living room
carpet.

'How are you, Barry?' said Nancy, coming over and curling her arm round my shoulder, but I just ignored her and carried on with what I was doing.

'I had a word with the director about the next advert. He said we could do it on skateboards!' smiled Bunky, as if we were still best friends, and I mouthed 'Yay!' and waggled my hands all sarcastically.

doesn't realise I'm being sarcastic

sarcastic waggling

I flumped down at my desk and started drawing insects in my notebook. 'I don't want to be in your evil nit-murdering adverts,' I mumbled, writing 'NITS ARE THE KEELEST' in my best capitals at the top of a new page.

Just then, Darren barged through the classroom doors on his roller skates. 'Helloooo, Darren fans!' he burped, holding up a phone and pressing play on the screen.

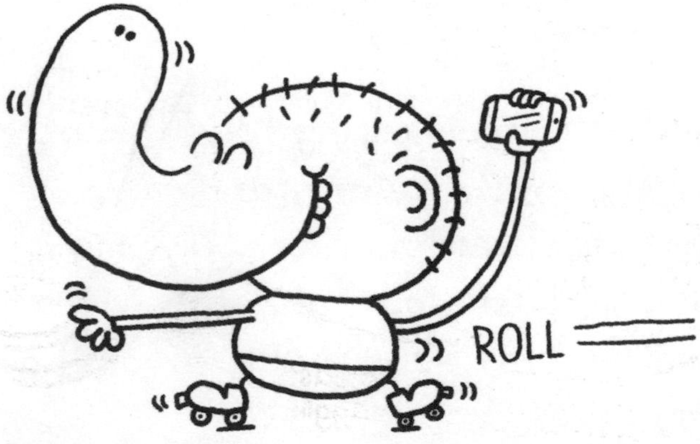
ROLL

I squinted my eyes and saw him, Bunky and Nancy gliding down the posh street, high fiving each other and acting like they were the keelest people ever. 'FEEKO'S NIT SHAMPOO KILLS NITS DEAD!' growled a voice at the end of the advert, and everyone cheered.

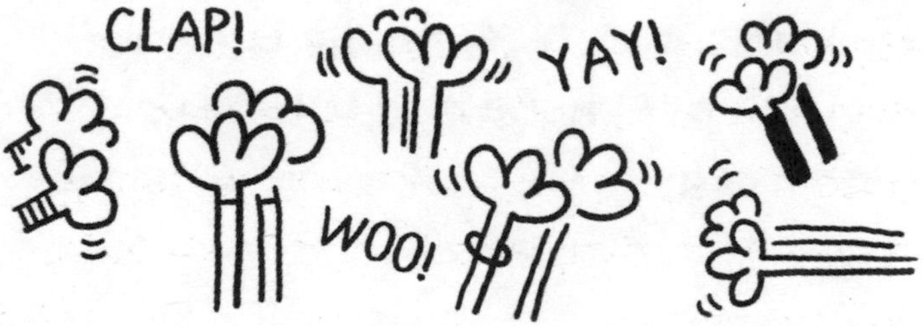
CLAP!
YAY!
WOO!

'What are you cheering for?' I shouted, scraping my chair and standing up. 'These people are murdering innocent nits!' I sat back down and drew a woodlouse, my hand shaking from how angry I was.

'He's gone stark raving bonkers!' laughed Darren, pressing play on the phone screen to make the advert start again. 'If anyone wants my autograph, I'm signing people's faces this lunchtime in the playground!'

A fly that'd been buzzing against the classroom window bonked his nose straight into the glass one last time and fell to the floor, dead from nose-bonk. I rolled my eyes, snapping a mini gravestone off a lolly stick in my pocket.

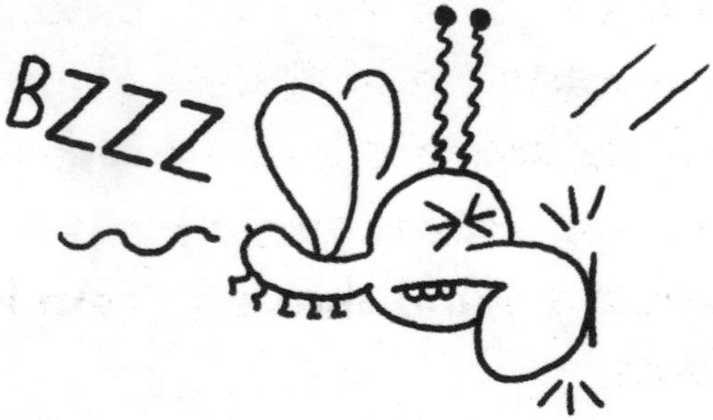
BZZZ

'Psst! Barry!' whispered Sharonella as I bent down to pick up the fly. 'I know you've gone mad and everything but I just wanted to say that I'm here for you, OK?'

I wasn't listening to her though. I was too busy coming up with one of my brilliant and amazekeel plans.

BZZZ ~

Give a bug a hug

The queue for autographs caterpillared all the way round the playground like one of those insects with twenty trillion legs I can never remember the name of.

'One at a time, Darren fans!' burped Darren, signing Fay Snoggles's nose, and Bunky snortled, scribbling his stupid name in someone's autograph book underneath Nancy's.

'Ready?' I said to Sharonella, taking a deep breath and accidentally breathing in a mosquito.

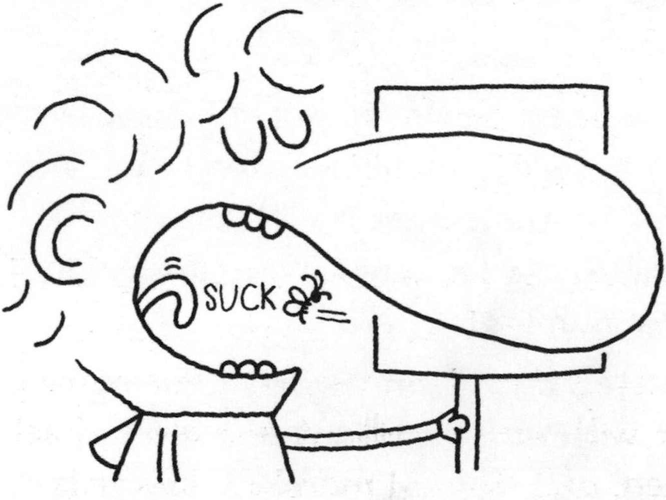
SUCK

'Huh? Oh yeah, I was born ready!' said Sharonella, who was standing next to me picking her nose and holding a poster with 'NITS ARE PEOPLE TOO!' written on it.

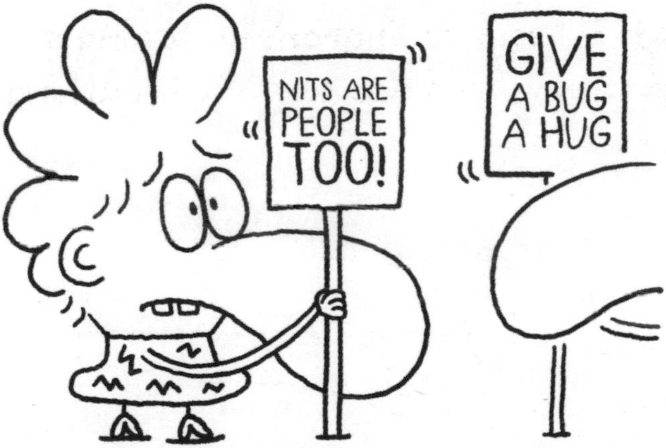
NITS ARE PEOPLE TOO!
GIVE A BUG A HUG

I looked at my poster, which said 'GIVE A BUG A HUG' in my biggest capitals, patted myself on the back for coming up with such a brilliant and amazekeel idea, and started marching towards my ex-best-friends.

'Ban Feeko's Nit Shampoo!' I shouted, waving my poster in the air and hitting a ladybird but not killing it, so that's OK.

'GIVE-A-BUG-A-HUG,' burped Darren, reading my poster out loud. 'OK!' he snortled, running towards a daddy-long-legs that was flying past, minding its own business. 'Come to daddy, Daddy!' he snarfled, grabbing it by the wings and giving it a cuddle.

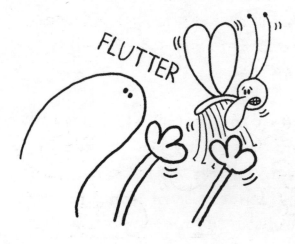

FLUTTER

'NOOO!!!' I screamed, dropping my poster and running towards him. Darren opened his arms and the daddy-long-legs dropped to the floor, all dizzy. 'You almost killed him!' I cried, stroking its wings, and it floated off, a bit wobbly.

'Oh no, I'm about to tread on an anty-want!' said Darren in a baby voice, lifting his foot above an ant that was strolling past. I scrabbled towards it on my hands and knees and scooped it up just in time.

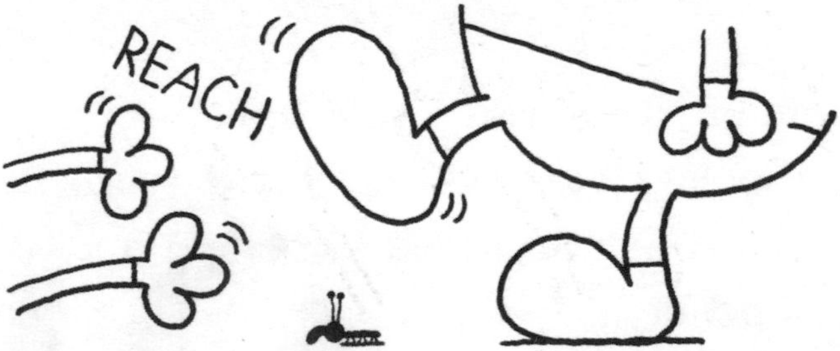
REACH

The ground shook as Darren's foot stomped on to the floor, or maybe it was Mrs Dongle the school secretary bounding over.

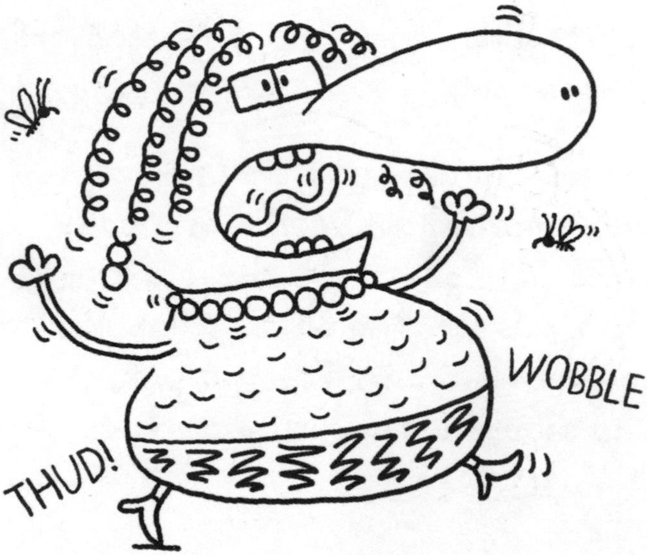
WOBBLE
THUD!

'Boys, boys, I cannot tolerate this tomfoolery!' she wheezed, the wooden beads on her necklace knocking against each other.

'He started it!' burped Darren, opening
a can of Fronkle and slurping it down
in one go.

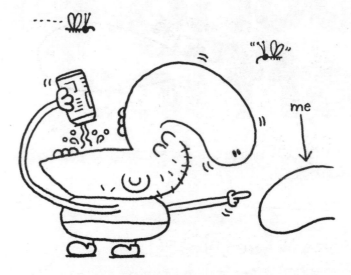

me

Mrs Dongle looked at me, lying on the
floor holding an ant, then over at my
poster. 'GIVE A BUG A HUG,' she said,
reading it out loud. 'That's perfect!'

Mrs Dongle's office

It was ten minutes later and I was in Mrs Dongle's office, but not because I'd been naughty or anything.

'Have you heard about Mogden Common, Barry?' she smiled, offering me a chocolate digestive.

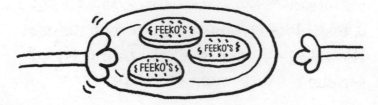

'Yes,' I said, but it came out as 'Mmf' because of the chocolate digestive I'd just stuffed in my mouth. 'It's that bit of grass where all the dogs do their poos,' I mumbled, spraying crumbs all over her desk.

Mogden Common

'That's it!' she chuckled. 'It's one of the last natural parts of Mogden left. Did you know that Feeko's wants to build a brand new mini supermarket right in the middle of it?' she said, suddenly all serious.

I thought of Mogden Common and remembered Mr Fly, lying in his tiny grave. 'I HATE Feeko's,' I said, looking out the window at Bunky and Nancy, acting all keel because of their stupid Feeko's advert.

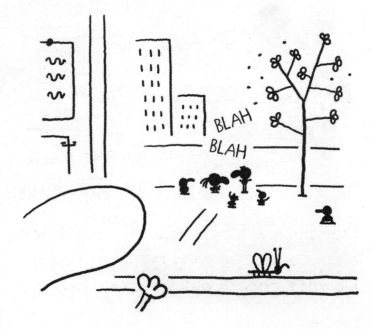

'There's a protest march coming up to stop them building it,' said Mrs Dongle, passing me another digestive, and I started to realise why the ground shook when she ran. 'Your posters would add just the FIZZAZZ we need!'

I slotted the biscuit into my mouth like a coin into a vending machine, and a blowoff popped out the other end.

The Feeko's protest

I spent the whole rest of the week making posters for Mrs Dongle, and burying insects I'd accidentally killed, and not telling Sharonella about the Feeko's protest, otherwise she'd want to come too.

Then all of a non sudden it was Saturday and I was standing on the edge of Mogden Common with Mrs Dongle and all her wooden-bead-necklace friends and their husbands, wondering how in the unkeelness my life had ended up so loserish.

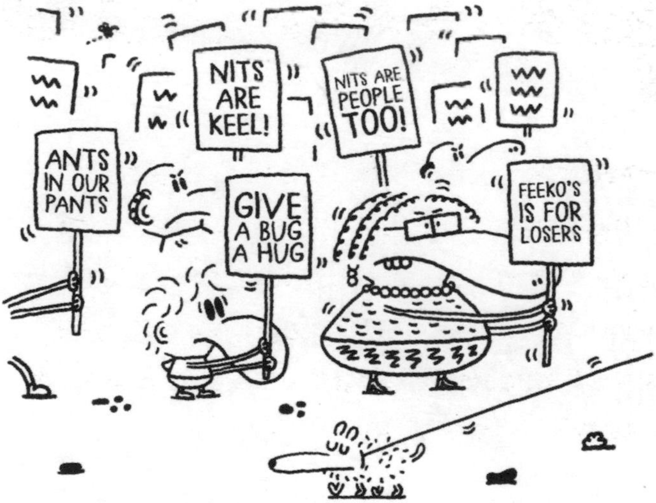
NITS ARE KEEL!
NITS ARE PEOPLE TOO!
ANTS IN OUR PANTS
GIVE A BUG A HUG
FEEKO'S IS FOR LOSERS

'Boo Feeko's!' growled an old granny, doddering past with a pram full of sausage dogs. She pulled a tied-up plastic bag out of her pocket and threw it at the enormous billboard that had been put up the day before.

THROW

'YOUR NEW FEEKO'S FUNSIZE WILL BE HERE SOON!' said the billboard in the biggest capitals ever, and I wondered if me and Mrs Dongle's friends were wasting our time with our tiny little posters.

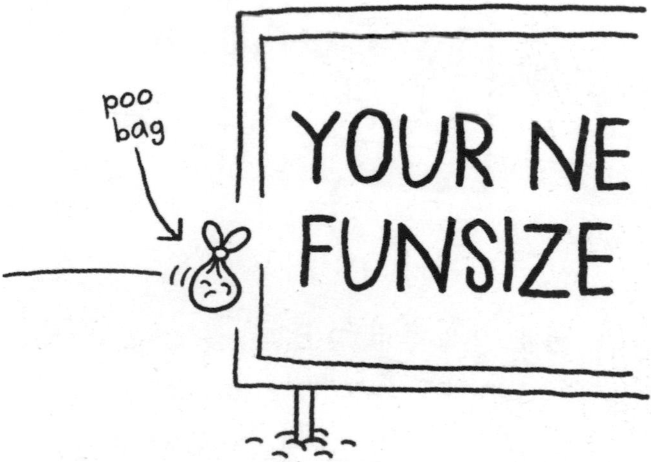
poo bag
YOUR NE
FUNSIZE

'Yes, that's right, Boo Feeko's!' shouted Mrs Dongle, waving her poster. On it I'd written 'FEEKO'S IS FOR LOSERS', which wasn't my most genius idea ever, but she seemed to like it.

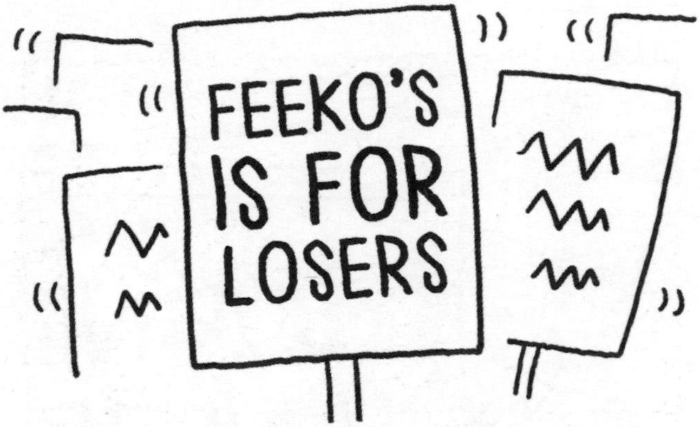
FEEKO'S
IS FOR
LOSERS

A van with a satellite dish on the roof and 'Mogden TV' written on its side screeched up. A man with a camera jumped out, followed by a lady with blonde hair and a microphone.

'We are live at Mogden Common, where a riot has broken out in protest against the new Feeko's Funsize!' she said, flicking her fringe like me when I had my bouncy hair for the audition.

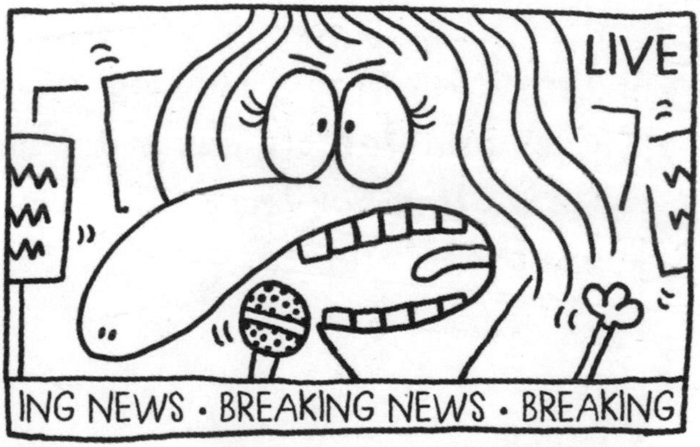
LIVE
ING NEWS • BREAKING NEWS • BREAKING

I looked around at all the Mrs Dongles and their husbands, standing there eating sandwiches and drinking tea.

Over on the other corner of the common, three figures started to glide towards us. One looked like a dog crossed with a human, the other had a cat's tail growing out of her head, and the third was half crocodile, half fat little belly.

I zoomed my eyes in and realised it was Bunky, Nancy and Darren, out practising their roller skating for the next evil nit-killing shampoo advert.

GLIDE

The cameraman swivelled round and started to film. 'This is verrry interesting,' said the blonde lady. 'It seems the stars of the huuuugely successful Feeko's Nit Shampoo advert have turned up. Who knows what could happen next?'

TREMBLE
MOGDEN NEWS
SHAKE

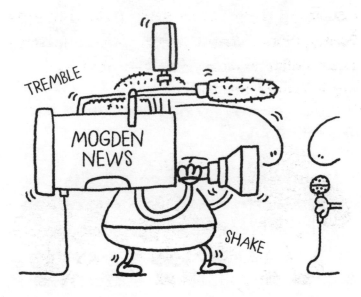

What happened next

'It's those nit shampoo kids!' shouted the old granny, giving her pram a push and letting go.

It zoomed off like me on roller skates, slicing a worm in half with one of its wheels. 'Get 'em, boys!' she cackled, and the dogs leaped out of the pram and ran towards Bunky like a string of sausages.

'ARRGGHHH!!!' screamed Bunky, who's
COM-PER-LEET-ER-LY scared of dogs.
He twizzled round to zoom off and
fell straight down on his bum. The
sausage dogs swarmed round him,
wagging their tails and yapping.

not really
a sausage

YAP!

WAG!

Mrs Dongle dropped her poster and
bounded over. 'Bad doggies, naughty
pooches!' she warbled, the TV people
right behind her.

'Tell us how you're feeling!' said the blonde lady, stuffing her microphone into Bunky's face.

'My bum hurts,' said Bunky, a sausage dog licking his face.

I tiptoed over and watched from behind my poster, hoping they wouldn't see me.

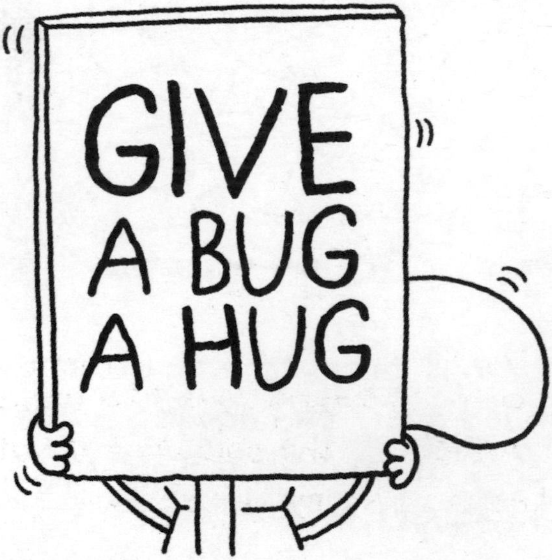
GIVE
A BUG
A HUG

'Well, well, if it isn't Barry Loser!' burped Darren, spotting me straight away, probably because of my massive nose sticking out from behind the poster. 'How many ants have you snogged today?' he laughed.

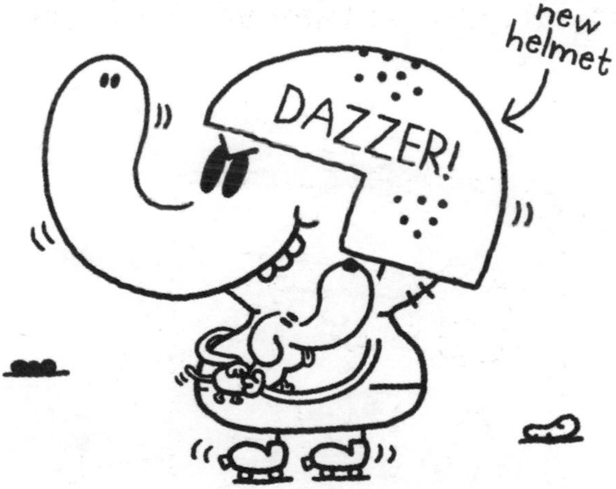
new helmet
DAZZER!

The camera swung round to me and I felt myself go the colour of a bottle of Feeko's Cherry Shampoo.

'How many have you KILLED, insect murderer?' I shouted, waving my poster and hitting a daddy-long-legs but not killing it, so that's OK.

'None yet, but it's never too late!' said Darren, grabbing a fly that was flying past, and all the Mrs Dongles and their husbands gasped.

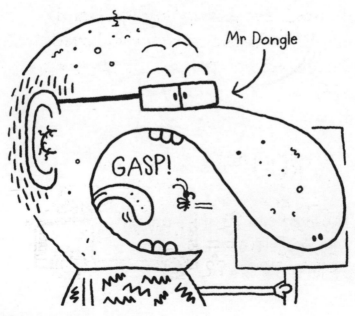

Mr Dongle

'Truly shocking scenes here at Mogden Common,' said the blonde lady into the camera. 'That was one of the stars of the Feeko's Nit Shampoo advert happily murdering a fly, just for the fun of it. This is Sandy Sandals for Mogden News Tonight!'

Darren opened his hand and the fly flew off, dizzily. 'Look! He's alive!' he shouted, but it was too late. Sandy Sandals and the cameraman were getting into their van and zooming off.

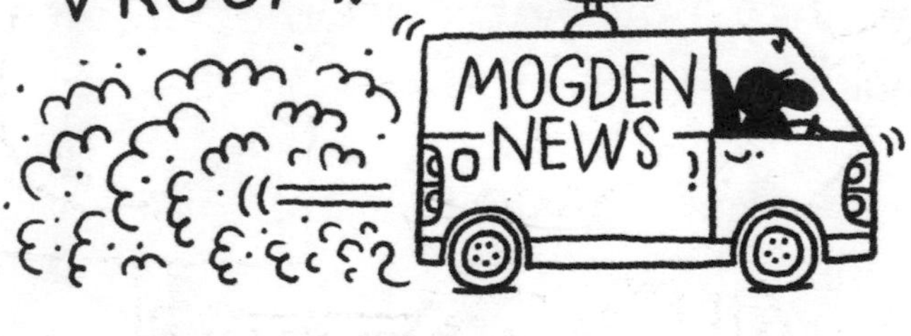
VROOM!
MOGDEN NEWS

The news

'Bazza, have you heard?!' screamed Sharonella as I skateboarded through the school gates on Monday morning.

'What, have I heard your VOICE?' I said, chuckling to myself about my own joke, not that I was in much of a chuckling mood.

'No, the news about Darren!'

I flipped my skateboard up and took my helmet off, scratching my head because all of a sudden I'd been feeling a bit itchy.

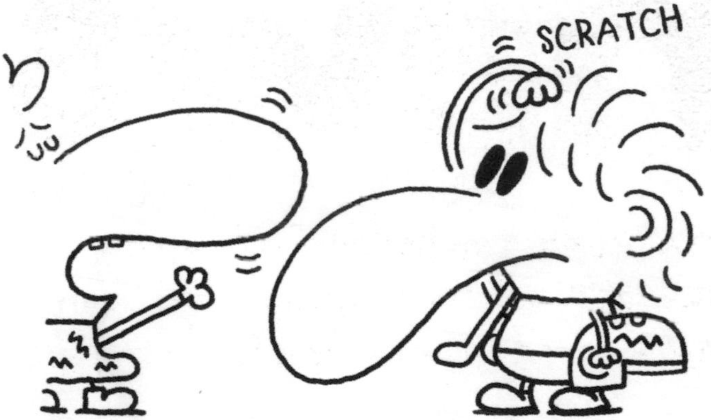
SCRATCH

'Feeko's fired him!' snortled Sharonella. 'Nancy and Bunky too! They saw what Darren did on Mogden News and said they couldn't have insect murderers in their nit shampoo adverts!'

I was just about to do my dance that makes my trousers fall down when I spotted Bunky walking through the school gates with Nancy and Darren.

'I suppose you're happy now, aren't you,' mumbled Bunky all sadly, scratching his head.

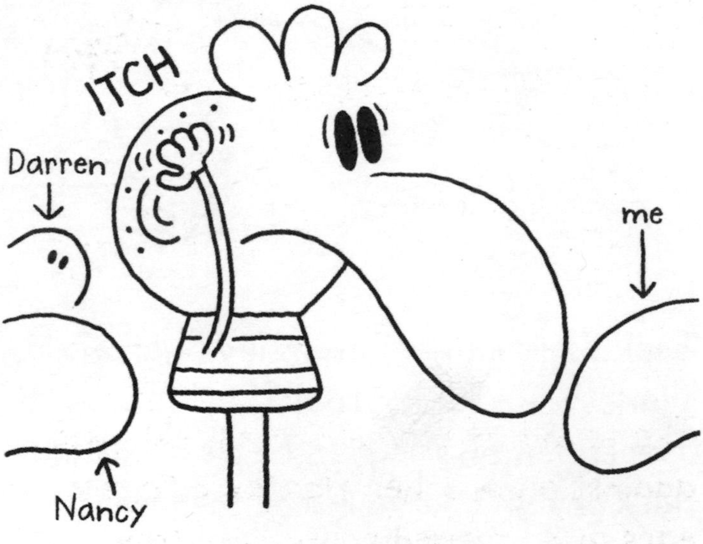
ITCH
Darren
me
Nancy

'Not really,' I mumbled back, because I wasn't really. I still hadn't been in a Feeko's Nit Shampoo advert, plus I didn't have any friends apart from Sharonella and the insects, not that they counted if I was being honest, which I was.

CLANG! CLONK! DONK!

CLANK! CLUNK!

The sound of wooden beads clanging against each other floated into my ears and I turned round and saw Mrs Dongle.

'Have you heard the news, Barry?' she warbled, and I scratched my head while shaking it. 'Our little protest was a complete waste of time. Didn't do anything! They're still going to build that ghastly Feeko's Funsize!'

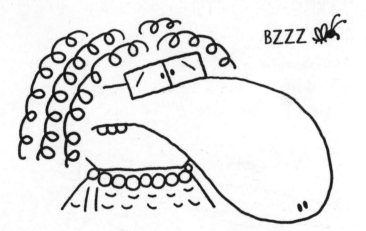

BZZZ

I did my sad face, mostly just to make Mrs Dongle happy, and carried on standing there, scratching my head. And then it happened.

Nits

'ARRGGHHH!!! NITS!!!' screamed
Mrs Dongle all of a sudden, pointing
at my hair, and she jumped and ran
off, her wooden beads clanging.

WAGGLE

'What is it? WHAT IS IT?' I cried, even
though Mrs Dongle had said what it
was.

Sharonella tiptoed over and peered into my hair. 'OH. MY. DAYS! Barry, you've got like a kazillion nits!' she said, squirming away from me and running off, screaming.

ZOOM!

I reached out to Nancy, forgetting we weren't friends any more, which is what happens when you're too busy worrying about all the nits eating away at your brain.

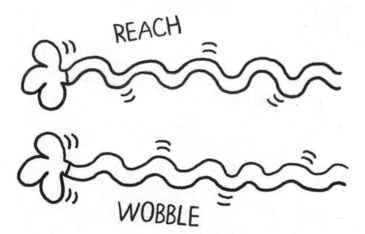

REACH

WOBBLE

'Nancy, you've got to help me!' I wailed, my legs and arms flailing.

Nancy slinked away from me, scratching her head, and I zoomed my eyes in and spotted the most nit-looking thing I've ever seen, going for a morning stroll along her eyebrow.

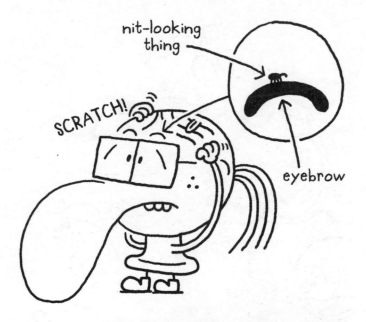

nit-looking thing

SCRATCH!

eyebrow

'ARRGGHHH!!! NITS!!!' I screamed, pointing at Nancy, and she started scratching and flailing, just like me.

'ARRGGHHH!!!! NITS!!!!' screamed Darren all of a sudden, pointing at Bunky's hair, and Bunky joined in with me and Nancy, itching himself like a dog.

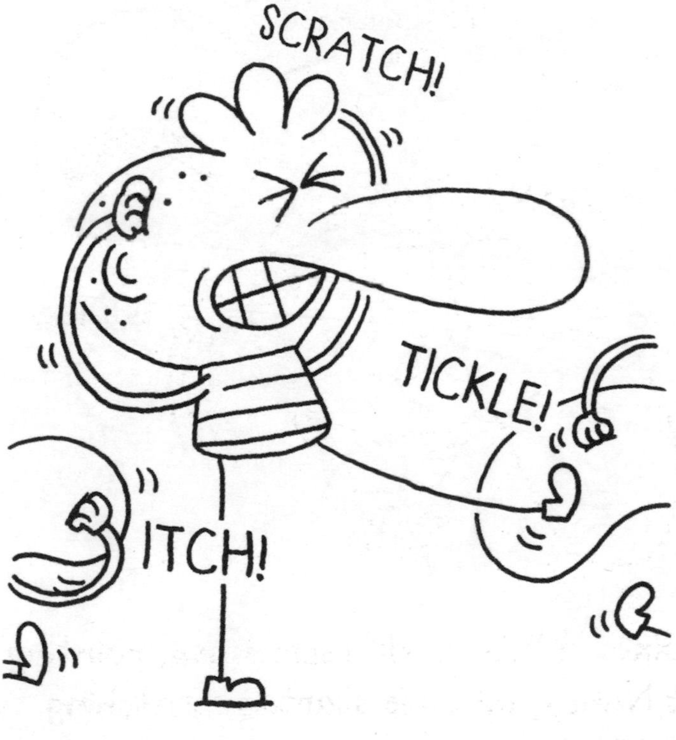
SCRATCH!
TICKLE!
ITCH!

'ARRGGHHH!!! NITS!!!' screamed Bunky, pointing at Darren, and that was how me, Bunky, Nancy and Darren all ended up standing in a circle doing the scratchy nit dance.

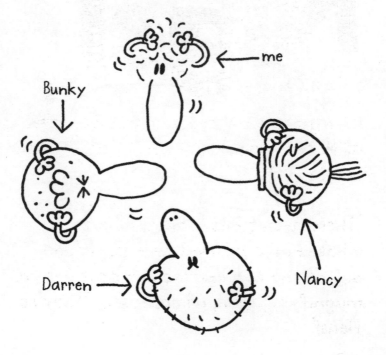

Nurse Nigel

It was ten minutes later and we were all in the nurse's room, but not because we had nits or anything.

'These aren't nits,' said the nurse, whose name is Nigel, tweezering one out of my ear and looking at it with a magnifying glass, all confused. 'They're fleas!'

I glanced over at Bunky, then Nancy, but not at Darren, because I don't really like looking at him all that much.

'The sausage dogs!' I laughed, remembering how one of them had been really scratching his bum with his mouth just before he'd licked Bunky's face.

Bunky's nose

flea

that dog

'Most extraordinary,' mumbled
Nurse Nigel to himself. He opened
his cupboard door and peered in,
scratching his chin, but not because he
had fleas or anything. 'Here we go!' he
smiled, pulling out a big plastic bottle
with 'Feeko's Flea Shampoo for Dogs'
written on it in massive non-capitals.

Nurse
Nigel

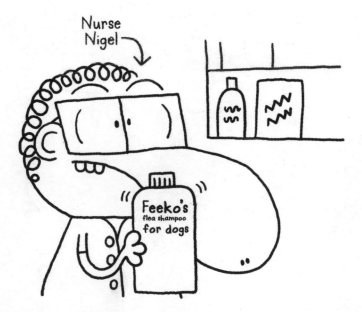

Feeko's
flea shampoo
for dogs

So that's how I ended up in the school showers with Bunky, Nancy and Darren, stripped to my **Future Ratboy** vest and pants and covered in Feeko's Flea Shampoo for Dogs.

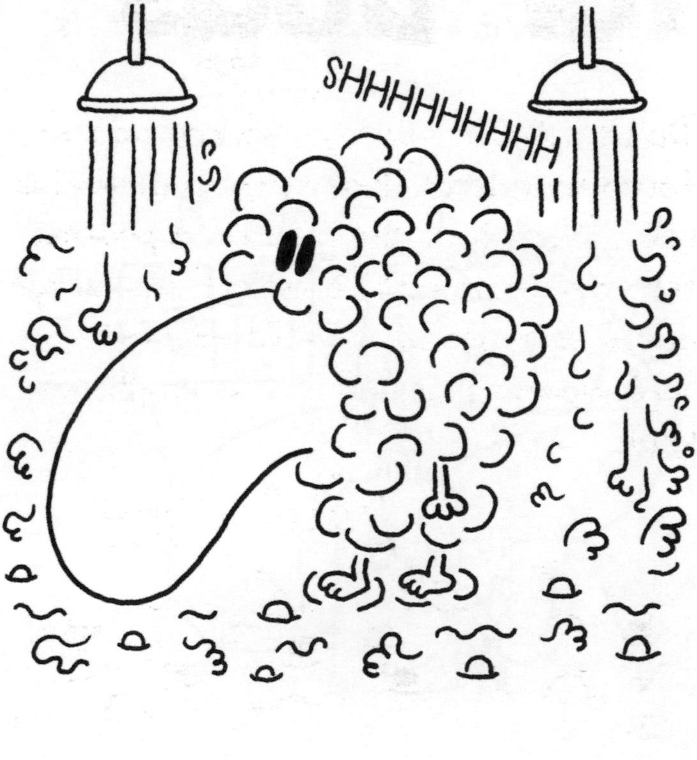
SHHHHHHHHHH

Feeko's Flea Shampoo for Dogs

'Do us a favour Barry,' burped Darren, foam and dead fleas running down his belly. 'Next time she goes on a protest, tell your mum not to bring her sausage dogs!' he snortled, and Nancy and Bunky giggled, trying not to laugh out loud.

foam bubble

dead flea

'She's YOUR mum, not mine!' I shouted, looking down at all the dead fleas floating in the water, feeling a bit bad because I'd gone back to being an insect killer like my evil ex-best-friends.

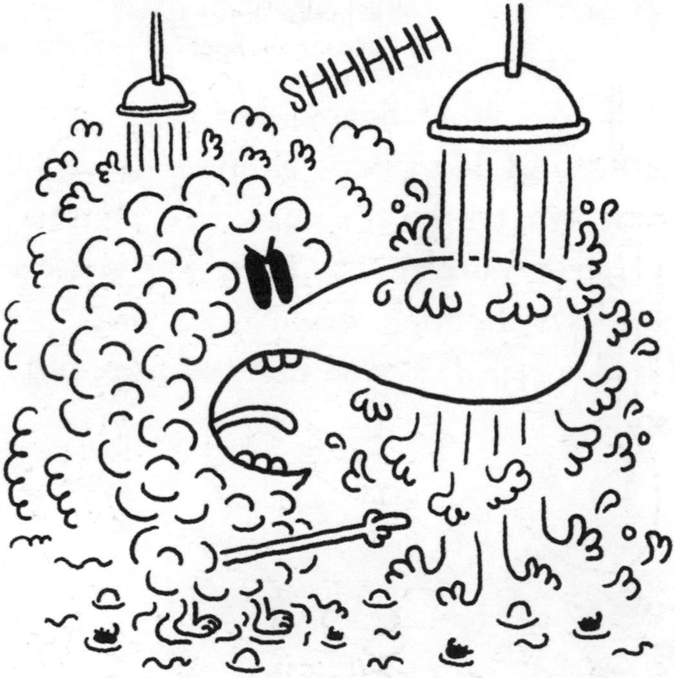
SHHHHH

'Get 'em, boys!' shrieked Nancy, doing her impression of the old granny with the pram, and I snortled to myself then stopped, because I was still angry with Bunky and Nancy for abandoning their leader.

looks like a toilet plunger taking off

'I'm sorry Barry, real-keely I am,' said Bunky, his whole head covered in flea shampoo foam. 'We shouldn't have done the advert without you.'

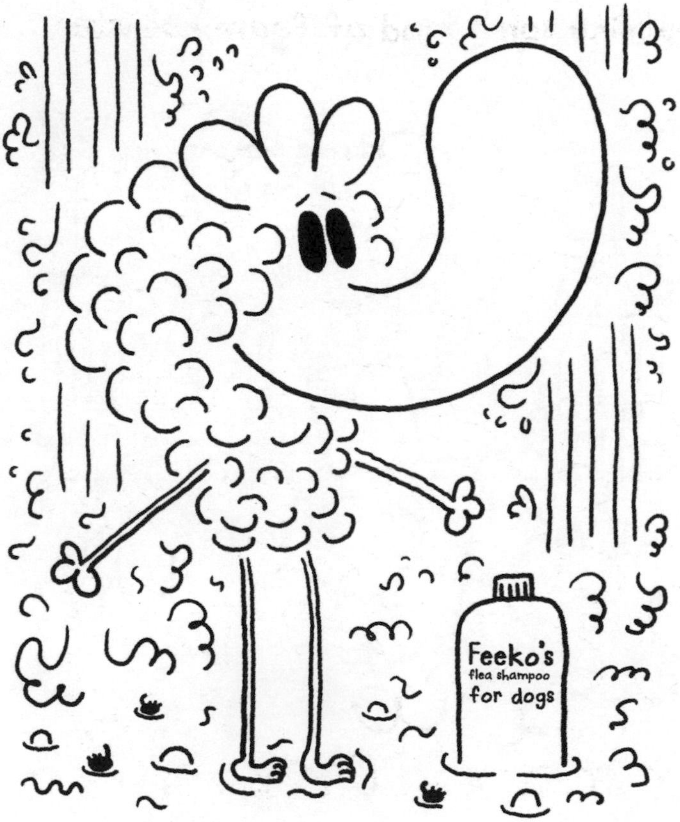
Feeko's
flea shampoo
for dogs

'Yeah, I don't know what came over us,' said Nancy, rubbing flea shampoo into her armpits. 'Pleeeaaassseee forgive us!' she groaned, staggering towards me with her arms stretched out like some kind of foam monster.

too much steam

'Yuck, I'm gonna be sick from all this niceness,' said Darren, and I looked at the three of them covered in flea shampoo and smiled, thinking how it would be keel if we were all in a Feeko's Flea Shampoo advert one day.

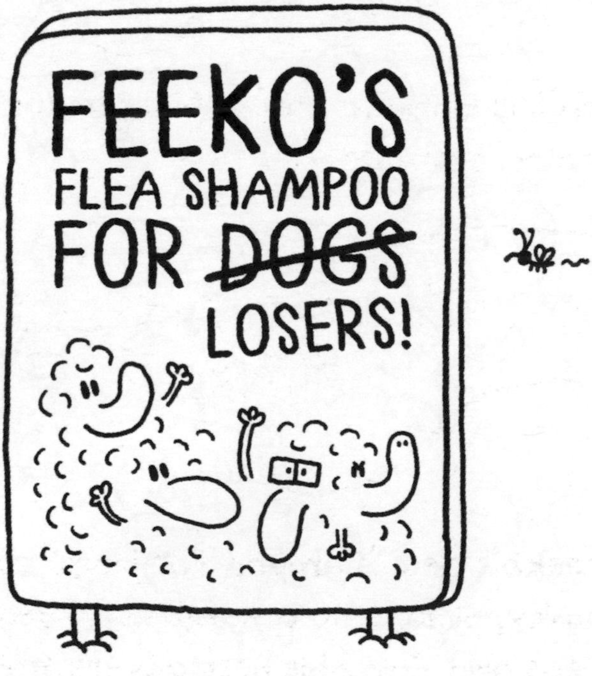
FEEKO'S
FLEA SHAMPOO
FOR ~~DOGS~~
LOSERS!

'What a LUVVERLY day!' I beamed, grabbing a handful of foam and squodging it into Nancy's head.

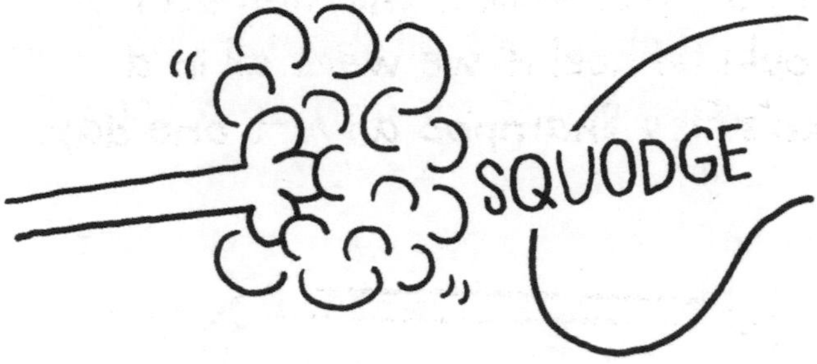
SQUODGE

'Isn't it glorious!' smiled Nancy, bonking me on the nose.

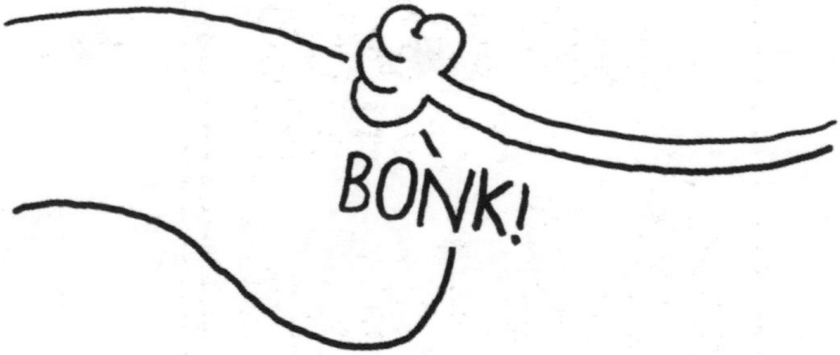
BONK!

'Feeko's Flea Shampoo for Dogs!' said Bunky, picking up a handful of dead fleas and doing his best advert smile.

I put my arms round him and Nancy,
and Darren too, because I was in a
good mood all of a sudden.

'It's the keelest!' we all shouted, but we
didn't jump in the air and do a little
dance, because that's extremely
dangerous when you're in or around
water. Plus I didn't want my pants
to fall down.

The endy-poos.

Now draw some bugs.

That is an order.

Loserfact ④

Jim Smith had nits about three times when he was a kid. One time when he had them and was looking in the mirror, he saw one carrying its dead friend along the top of his eyebrow.

LOSERFACT

5

Jim Smith's first school trip was to the Isle of Wight. He got in trouble on the first day for turning his ring pull into a flying saucer, which is something you could do with the old-fashioned types of ring pulls. This makes it sounds like Jim was a naughty boy, but he wasn't, he was a very good boy indeed.

UFO

old ringpull

ADVIRT

Coffee is gross.

Except your mums & dads are all addicted.

Cafe Cafe

15 Mogden High Street

My 10 Keelest questions EVER!

Here are the winners of my 'keel questions' competition. It was a competition where people sent in keel questions, and the top ten keelest ones got printed in this book. Enjoykeels!

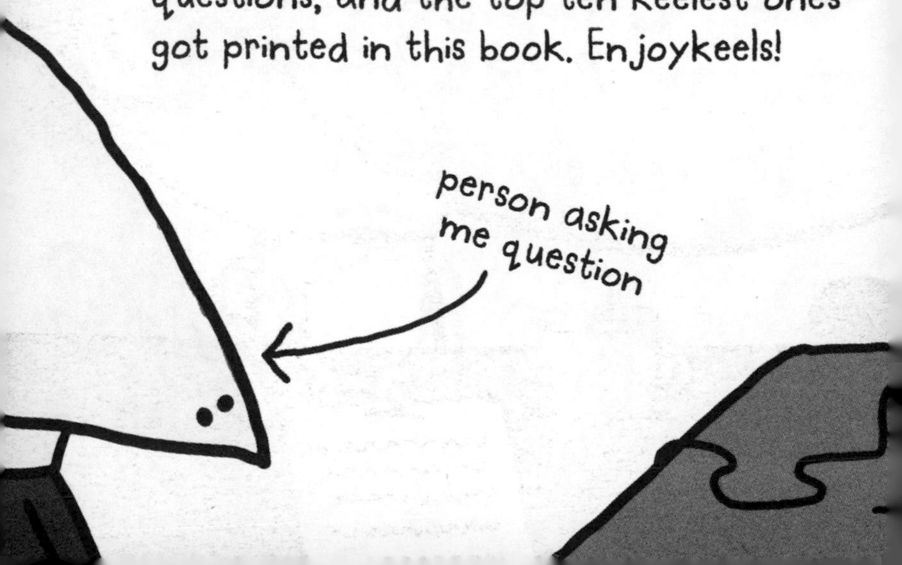
person asking me question

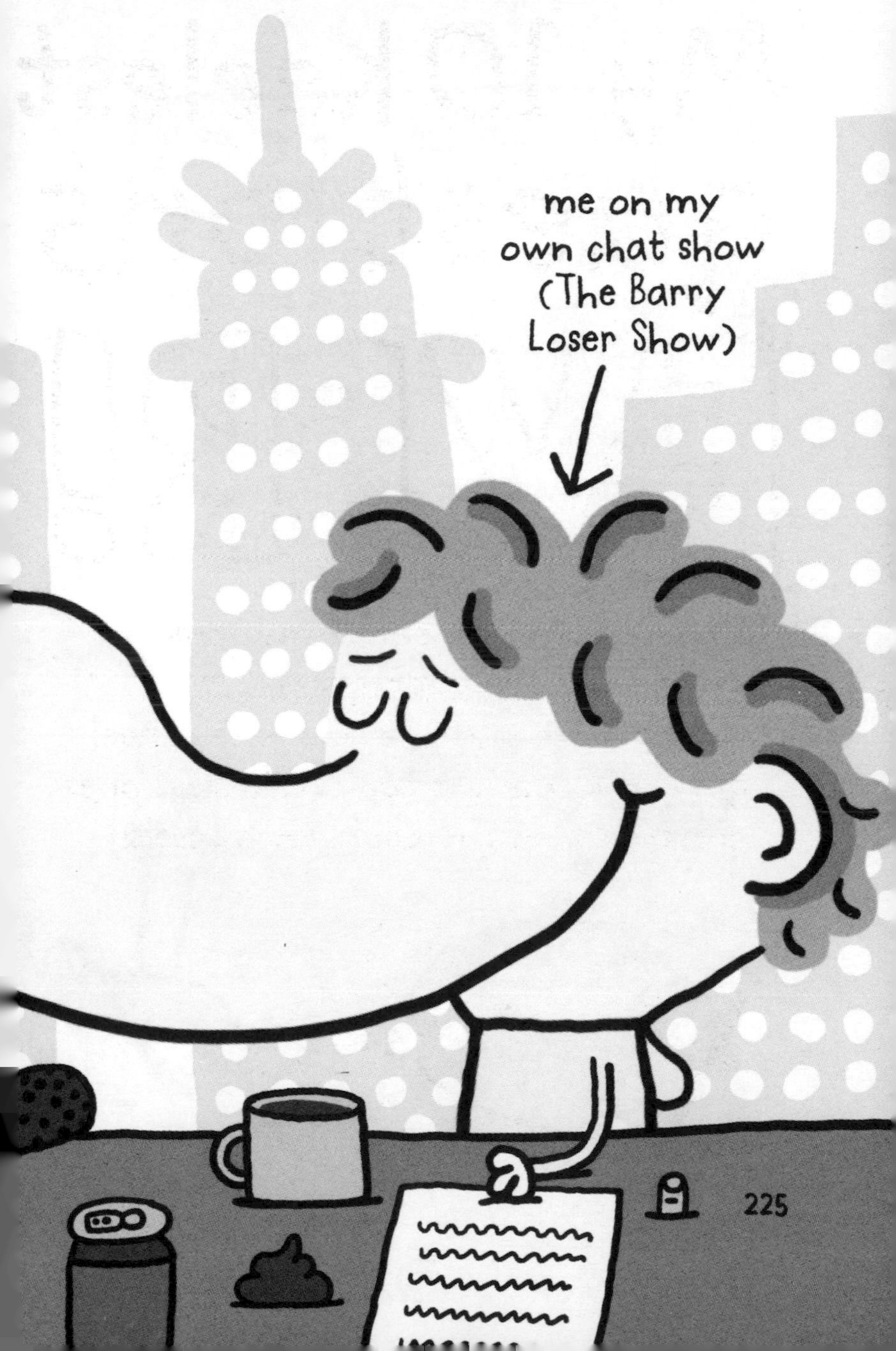
me on my
own chat show
(The Barry
Loser Show)

GABE: Dear Barry, what ever happened to snailypoos?

Good morning Gabe, good question. Snailypoos is still alive, and now has nine hundred and seventy three children. We met up for a can of Fronkle just the other day, and apart from how tired he looks these day's, he's just the same.

JACOB: Dear Jim, Can you ask Barry what was the hardest nose bonk he ever received?

Good evening Jacob, I've just been on the phone to Barry and he says the hardest nose bonk he's ever received was from Anton Mildew's invisible friend Invis. Barry didn't even know it'd happened until Anton told him. That's why it was so hard - because it didn't even make sense. I mean, how can an invisible friend bonk your nose? (When I say hard, I mean hard to work out, by the way).

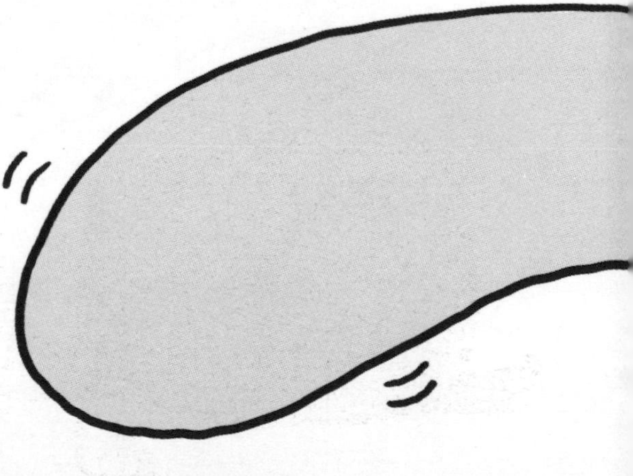

AISHA: Dear Jim, What shoe size is Barry Loser?

Hi Aisha, shoe sizes are different in Mogden - all shoes come in Keel, Keeler and Keelest. Barry's shoe size is Keelest.

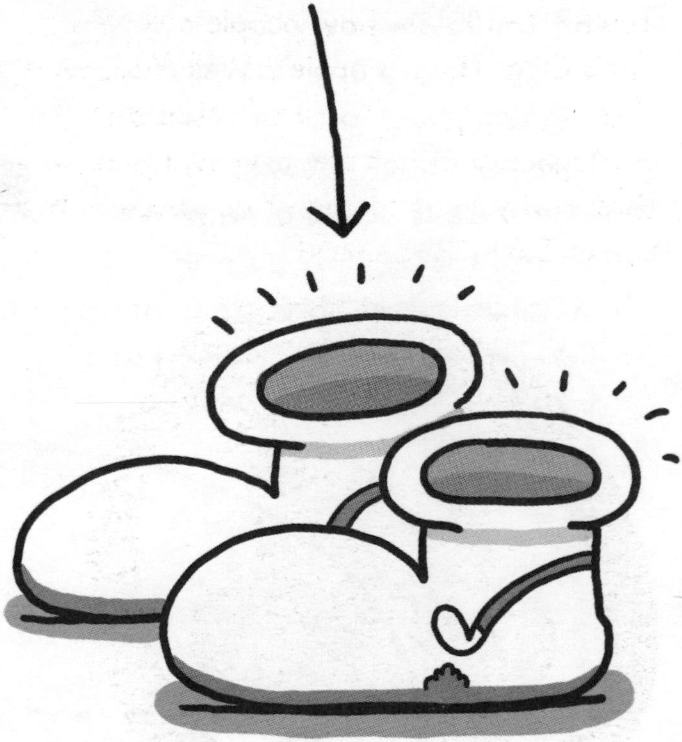

JIM'S EDITOR: Dear Jim, can you please stop putting so many poos in your books? I feel a bit sick.

Dear Liz, Let me explain why I put so many poos in my books. Did you know that dog poos are sort of like the logo for Mogden Town? You know how people call New York City 'The big apple'? Well Mogden is 'The big dog poo'. You can't step one step in Mogden without stepping in a poo. So that's why I put so many dog poos in my books. Sorry not sorry!

HAZEL: Hi Jim, Are your books for a special purpose or do you just like making them?

Hi Hazel, I've always liked making books. In fact, I have a box of little books I made all for myself that hardly anyone else apart from me ever sees.

LILY AMBER: Dear Jim, What is the most embarrassing thing that's ever happened to you?

Hi Lily Amber, I once pooed myself at the beach in Lee Bay, North Devon when I was a kid. I was in my swimming trunks and had to walk back to the hotel room with my bum up against the wall the whole way so no-one would notice. Beaches always used to make me need a poo. And libraries. I've told you the exact spot it happened in so you can visit it and imagine the scene better.

Jim

MORGAN: Dear Barry, When did you do your biggest blowoff and why?

Morgan, this is a very important question. My biggest ever blowoff was when me and Bunky were running away from Mrs Trumpet Face's house after we'd knocked on her door. I'd been saving up the blowoff for three years, and now was the perfect time to use it! Its turbo powers helped me escape down an alleyway at superkeelness speed. Unfortunately the blowoff blew straight into Bunky's face and he fainted and was captured by the evil Mrs Trumpet Face, then taken back to her dungeon where he still is now.

I just made that all up by the way.

ZUNAIR: Dear Jim, How do you get these mind blowing ideas?

Hi Zunair, I like your name. It's like you're an aeroplane company. The answer to your question is in your question - I 'get' them - I don't look for them, they just pop up and I take them. Although you have to know when they've popped up I spose. I think mostly it's just that I'm really bored most of the time, so I try to entertain myself with whatever's going on inside my brain.

you

ZUNAIR

ARCHIE: Dear Barry, What's your favourite part about Not Bird?

Hi Archie, my favourite part about Not Bird is the little washing-instructions tag that sticks out of his bum. I'm talking about my cuddly Not Bird, of course. Although the real Not Bird also has a washing-instructions tag. I wish I had one of those sticking out of my bum, then I'd know what temperature to wash myself at.

keel!

DANIEL: Hi Barry! Will you ever marry Nancy Verkenwerken?

Hi Daniel, who knowkeels! Maybe we could get married in one of my books, and have Bunky as our baby. Did you know that Nancy Verkenwerken is actually based on Jim Smith's childhood pen-friend Nancy Vankeerbergen?

Funimals!

My dad used to play this game millions of years ago when he was a kid because there was nothing else to do. It's actually kind of keel - all you have to do is think of two animals then squidge them together.

Dog + Crocodile =
CROCODOGODILE

Pig + Slug = PLUG!

you draw it ↓

Puma + Unicorn

 +

= PUMICORN

Kangaroo + Jellyfish

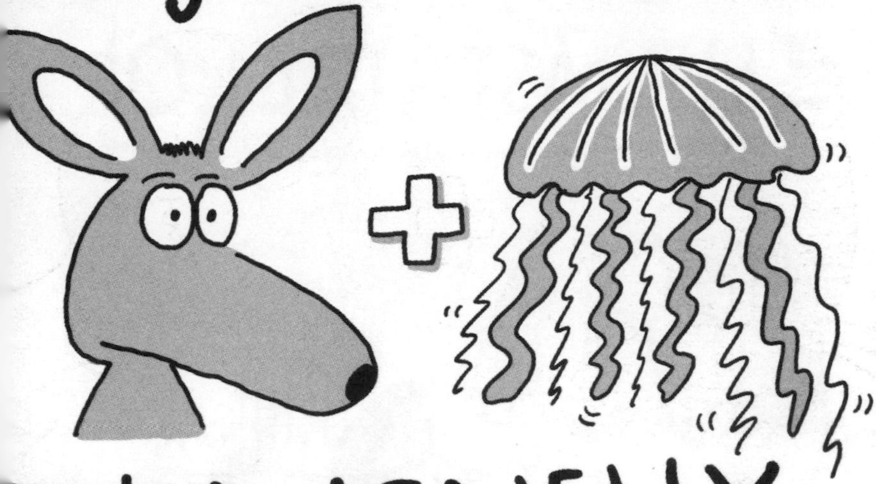

= KANGAJELLY

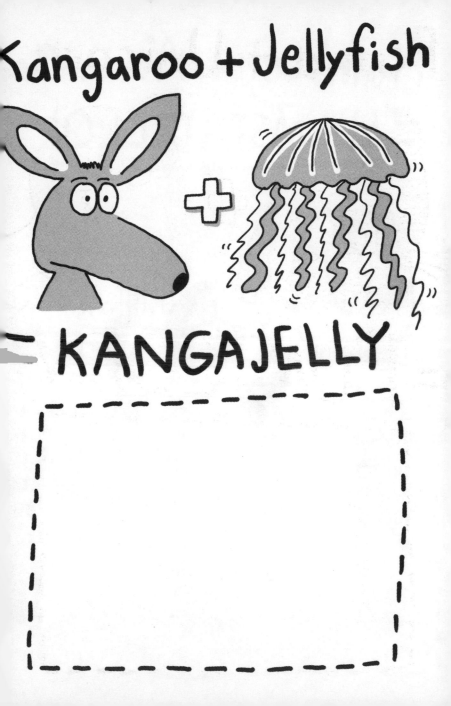

Hamster + Armadillo
= <u>HAMSTADILLO!</u>

Cat + Sloth = CLOTH

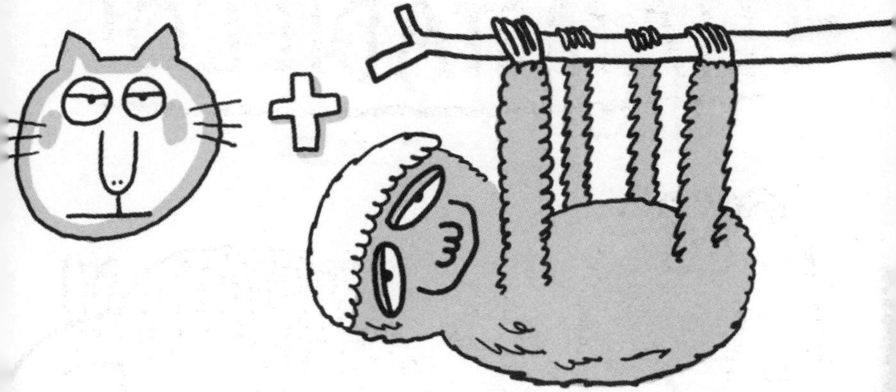

Dear Sharonella

Bit of a crazy letter this month, Shazfans...

HELPINGTONS!!!!
I'VE BEEN TRANSPORTED
10 MILLION YEARS INTO...
THE FUTURE!!!

I'M LIVING IN A BIN OUTSIDE A
FEEKO'S SUPERMARKET... APART FROM
FEEKO'S IS NOW CALLED 'FREEKO'S'!

2 DAYz LATER...
ME AGAIN! THIS BIN **STINKS**!
THE KEEL THING IS, IT'S A HOVER-
BIN. EVERYTHING IS HOVER HERE IN
THE FUTURE! ANYWAY, CAN YOU
RECOMMEND A GOOD HAT FOR STOPPING
RUBBISH GETTING IN YOUR HAIR? ALSO, HOW
DO YOU ACTUALLY 'GET OUT' OF A BIN??!!
PLUS DO YOU NEED ANYTHING FROM FREEKO'S
WHILE I'M HERE? MAYBE SOME HOVER TOILET ROLL
OR A PINT OF MILK (HOVER OR SEMI-HOVER?)
SEEYA!! XXOXOX

Nan, is that you?
Oh my days, how
did THAT happen,
LOL? Anyway, what
about a bin lid over
your head? It'd
really go with the
bin. Although if it's a
hover bin lid it'll just
float off, LOLS. It's
just really hard to
know how to help.
Listen Nan, if there's
ANYthing I can DO
just say, yeah?

Shazzingtons
o-x-

ADVERT

KEEP PLAYING IT KEEL, LOSERS.

Keel. Keep playing it.

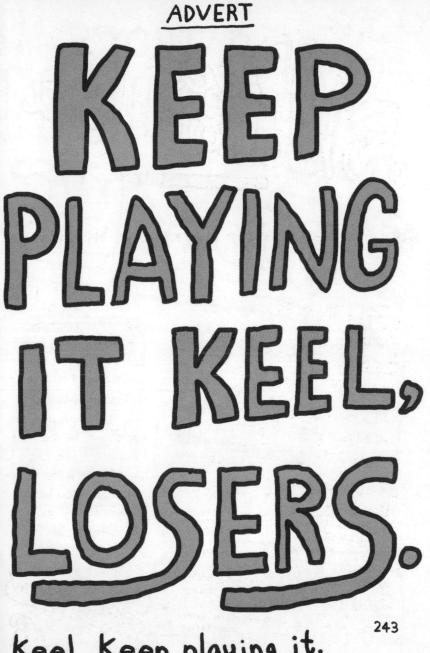

FUTURE RATBOY'S RUBBISH JOKES

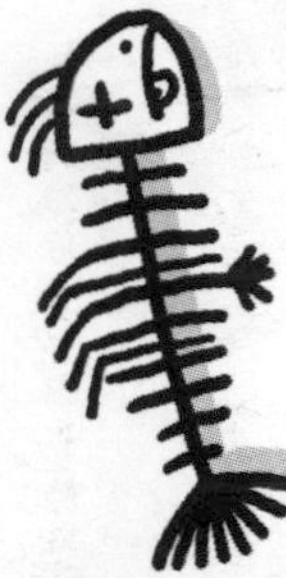

'They're rubbish!'

What do bins say to each other when they haven't seen each other for a while?

- Where you bin?

Did you see that TV show that's filmed in a bin?

It's rubbish!

WHICH BIN WENT TO THE SCHOOL DISCO?

- The GLITTER bin!

Did you see that OTHER TV show that's filmed in a bin?

It's LITTERally the best show ever!

Which bin has LOADS of opinions?
-The Twitter bin!
What do you do when you're bored of your bike?
RECYCLE IT.
I'm not groaning at all at these hilarious jokettes!
Did you hear about the bin that could do tricks?
He's WHEELIE good!!
LAUGHING SO MUCH RIGHT NOW.
Where do you take rubbish letters?
The com-post office!
Did you hear about the really fast recycling van?
It's bin & gone!
What do bins say to each other when they decide they're gonna stop being friends because they've run out of stuff to say?
"BIN NICE KNOWING YOU"

Design a superhero

Future Ratboy got zapped by lightning while he was inside a bin with his cuddly toy bird, an old TV set, and a rat.

That's how he ended up millions of years in the future as a half rat, half boy, half TV, with a cuddly flying bird as his sidekick.

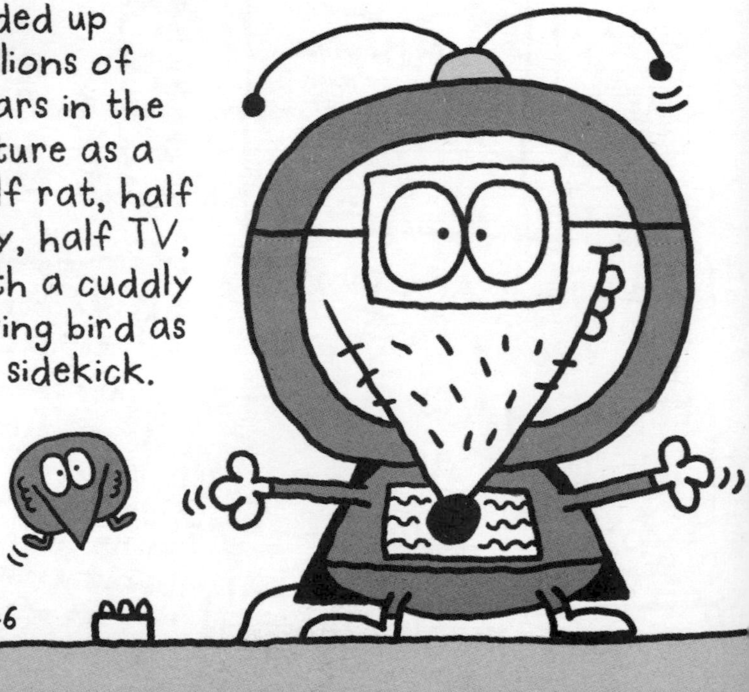

Use this page to come up
with your own superhero –
make sure you know how
they got their super powers,
and give them a sidekick.

↓

ADVERT
THE SHNOZINATOR 9000
Take a trip to the future!
SHNOZ-INATOR 9000!
IN FEEKO'S NOW!

Dear Sharonella

This week's letter comes from Mildred in Flopton, wherever that is...

Dear Sharonella,

You know how you're sposed to have a 'naughty step' for badly behaved children?

Well, I have a naughty step. Except I have no children. It's just a very naughty step.

Every time I go up or down the stairs and I step on the step, it makes a creaking noise that sounds like I'm doing a blow-off. I get ever so embarrassed, even though it's just me and Terry* these days.

Any advice?

Mildred x

*the tortoise

OH. MY. DAYS.

Mildred, you make me LARF!

That is SO funny, spesh that it's your tortoise you're worried about hearing you!

I say, enjoy your blowoffs!

That's what I say anyway!

Shaz
x

The Loser-fan quiz!

How much of a Barry fan are you? Find out by answering these ridikeelous questions...

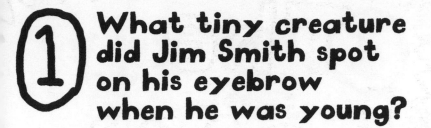

1 What tiny creature did Jim Smith spot on his eyebrow when he was young?

— — — — — — — —

2 What's the name of the shampoo Barry and friends advertised?

— — — — — — — —

 **What was the name of Jim Smith's best friend when he was young?**

– – – – – – – –

What does Barry tread in, like, ALL the time?

5 What sort of aunt is Sharonella?

- - - - - -

6 What did Jim Smith used to make old ring pulls into?

- - - - - - - -

7 How many fingers does Jim Smith draw Barry and his friends with?

- - - - - - -

8 What sweets does Dolly sell in her sweet shop?

- - - - - - -

9 Which friend of Granny Harumpadunk's has disgusting feet?

10 What's the name of Mogden School's newspaper?

ANSWERS: 1. Nit 2. Feeko's Nit Shampoo 3. Ben
4. Dog poo 5. Agony 6. Flying saucers 7. Three
8. Thumb Sweets 9. Ethel 10. The Daily Poo

Complaints

Thank you for reading my amazekeel book, I hope you liked it. If there were any bits you didn't like, please write them down on this page, then close the book and put it on a shelf.

\- - - - - - - - - - - - - - - -

\- - - - - - - - - - - - - - - -

\- - - - - - - - - - - - - - - -

\- - - - - - - - - - - - - - - -

\- - - - - - - - - - - - - - - -

\- - - - - - - - - - - - - - - -